CYNTHIA HICKEY

Drowned in Silence

Cynthia Hickey

The Sheriff of Misty Hollow, Book 4

ISBN-13: 978-1-965352-98-4

Prologue

The killer slipped through the trees like a wisp of smoke, each step rehearsed, each breath measured. The killer cannot make a mistake.

Tonight is the night. After days of observation and planning, the killer sees the victim, right where she should be. Abby Pearson hums along the shoreline, alone as usual. Foolish girl? Doesn't she know how dangerous it is?

The killer springs forward and blocks the girl's retreat. Abby gasps, confusion filling her eyes as she recognizes the face in front of her. Her brow furrows. Then, sensing that the usually friendly face now means her harm, she whirls to run. The killer clamps a gloved hand over her mouth. The pungent odor of ether soaked into the glove, filled the air. Not enough to keep her unconscious for long. The killer thirsts to feel the life drain from the girl's body.

The struggle is short. Abby slumps to the ground.

Gripping her under both arms, the killer dragged her to a waiting rowboat moored at the edge of the lake, concealed from the main trail by tall reeds. The killer pulled the girl into the water.

The coolness of the water revives Abby. The killer smiles and submerges her face below the surface of the lake. Abby's hands claw at the killer's arms, panic making her strength desperate. The killer holds her under, relishing in the frantic struggle—the bubbles, the trembling of her body. The girl's fight slows, then ceases. The moment her body goes slack, the killer steps back. The silence settles, cold and absolute.

After a few seconds of no movement, the killer drags the body into the boat and places the girl on her back. After smoothing her wet hair away from her face, the killer folded the girl's arms over her stomach. To the casual observer, Abby seems nothing more than a girl dozing, not a victim of violence.

The killer placed a small card under the folded hands before placing a silver heart necklace next to her side. "Foolish girl doesn't know the dangers of walking alone at night."

A gentle push of the killer's foot sends the boat away from the reeds. It drifted a short way along the misty water's edge before stopping the length of the rope, mooring it to the bank. As the boat drifted, the killer picked up a bucket on the shore and washed away the footprints.

Satisfied, the killer melted back into the trees, pausing once to watch the fog envelope the boat. A secret for now, but the dawn will reveal the horror waiting for the unsuspecting hiker.

Chapter One

Sheriff Shea Callahan crouched next to the rowboat that had drifted to shore, moored by a weathered rope. Her gaze flickered over details. The angle of the body, the scrape on her cheek, from the side of the boat maybe? She sighed and, planting her palms firm against her thighs, pushed to stand.

She noted the drag marks that suggested the body had been moved. A flash of white from the water's edge drew her attention. With a gloved hand, she pulled a white sneaker with daisies printed on the canvas from the weeds and placed it in a bag.

Deputy Trevor Bolton stood a few feet away, black rubber gloves on his hands as he sketched a rough diagram of the scene. "Identification," he nodded to a cell phone next to the body. "Says she's Abby Pearson. The parents have not been notified yet. Said their daughter went hiking last night. When she didn't return, they figured she'd spent the night with a friend. I bagged a necklace from next to her body."

The silver chain caught the morning light as Trevor held up the evidence bag, a small heart pendant visible through the plastic. Shea recognized it immediately—half the girls at the high school wore identical ones from the local jewelry store's discount bin.

"I see where the body was dragged, but what's strange is the fact that there are no footprints." Gaze on the ground, Shea moved away from the water's edge. A few strands of dark hair, Abby's, trembled from a low-hanging tree branch.

"Washed away." Trevor nudged a bucket half buried in the mud. "This was thought out, planned."

Shea knelt beside the bucket, studying its position. "Or covered up. Look at this—the mud's been disturbed around the rim, but there's no reason for that if it was just sitting here." She photographed the scene from multiple angles, her camera clicking steadily in the morning stillness.

"The killer could be watching us right now. Getting a thrill from the proceedings." Shea turned and surveyed the early morning forest. Mist still clung to the trees, creating ghostly shapes between the pines. "I want to talk to the ones who discovered the body."

"Two young boys." He jerked his head toward a battered Chevy pickup. "They're pretty shaken up."

The truck sat at an angle, as if the driver had pulled over hastily. Fishing rods jutted from the bed, and a tackle box rested on the tailgate. The boys sat in the front seat—one with his head in his hands, the other staring blankly at the lake.

Shea approached the two boys and spoke through the window. "I'm Sheriff Callahan. Can I have your names and what happened this morning?"

"That's our boat," one of them said, his words catching in his throat. His face was pale, freckles standing out like scattered pennies across his nose.

"He's Seth Reynolds," the other one said. "I'm Caleb Whittaker. We go fishing every Saturday morning. When we got here…we found…Abby."

"You knew her?"

They nodded in unison. "She's in our class. We're Juniors at the high school," Caleb said. "She sat behind me in history. Always borrowed a pen." His voice cracked on the last word.

"Does Abby usually go walking alone at night?"

Seth shrugged, wiping his nose with the back of his hand. "It's no secret that she likes to walk around the lake. Said it helps her think. We've got finals coming up, and she was stressed about college applications. Her mom wants her to go to the state university, but Abby wanted to study art somewhere smaller."

"The bucket yours?"

The boys nodded. "We use it for our catch," Caleb said. "Been using the same one for three years. My dad gave it to us when we started coming out here."

"Can you think of anyone who might have wanted to harm Abby?"

They shook their heads in unison, the movement mechanical, shocked.

"She was quiet, kind of shy, but well-liked." Caleb swallowed hard, his Adam's apple bobbing in his neck. "She helped tutor kids in art class. Never had a mean word to say about anyone."

"We'll have to take the boat and bucket as evidence. You'll get it back when we've finished our investigation." Shea handed them each a business card. "Call me if you think of anything that might be helpful, no matter how small."

Shea headed down the walking trail that circled the lake. In the distance, morning campfires flickered to life, sending thin columns of smoke into the gray sky. It had rained earlier yesterday, and she hoped the killer wouldn't have washed away any evidence on the trail. The path was soft underfoot, muddy in places where water had pooled.

She spotted footprints. One set matched the tread on Abby's shoe, the other the type you would find on the sole of hiking boots. She frowned. The boot prints weren't much larger than Abby's—either a small man or a woman.

About fifty feet from the lake, the tracks stopped at the base of a large pine. Shea brushed away the dead needles, finding a faint impression as if someone had crouched there. Waiting. The pine's thick trunk would have provided perfect cover, giving a clear view of the trail while remaining hidden.

She stood, tension tightening in her shoulders as she continued her search. There. A broken limb on a bush. Leaves disturbed. This was where Abby had fallen. The ground showed signs of a struggle—torn earth, scattered leaves, a small piece of blue fabric caught on a thorn.

How had the killer subdued her? Had the girl known her assailant and not suspected an attack? The struggle indicated Abby had fought back when she realized the danger.

She glanced back at the lake. The flashing lights of her patrol car highlighted the body of Abby, covered by a white sheet, Shea always kept in the back of her car. The sight never got easier, especially when the victim was so young. When the coroner from Langley arrived, Dr. Linda Fuller, Shea returned to the water's edge.

Dr. Fuller was a woman in her fifties with graying hair pulled back in a practical bun. She worked with quiet efficiency, her movements precise and respectful. "What do we have here?" she asked, pulling on latex gloves.

"Seventeen-year-old female, found in the boat this morning by two classmates. Appears to have been moved post-mortem."

The coroner glanced up. "I'm not busy. If you want to follow me back to the morgue, I can do the autopsy right now."

"Not being busy is a good thing." Shea exhaled slowly. In a county of their size, Dr. Fuller staying busy usually meant bad things were happening. "We'll follow you."

At the morgue, Shea and Trevor stood in the observation window. The sterile room felt cold despite the afternoon sun streaming through high windows. Arms folded, jaw tight, Trevor started to pace.

As Dr. Fuller worked, she called out her findings. "Time of death between ten and eleven p.m. Cause of death is drowning." She glanced at Shea through the glass. "I found a trace of ether in her nose. Not enough to knock her out for more than a few minutes, just enough to disorient her." She returned to the task at hand. "Defensive wounds, scrapes, and bruises showed she fought back. Skin beneath her fingernails."

"She fought," Shea said softly. "Good girl. Hopefully, the skin under her nails belongs to the killer, and the DNA is in our database."

"That would be too easy." Trevor stopped pacing and stared out the window. "Nothing's ever that simple in this job."

"Let's go question some campers. Maybe someone heard something."

"You okay?" It had been five months since their encounter with Troy, Trevor's murderous twin, and Trevor had only been back to work for two of those months. Some cases still hit him harder than others.

"I'm fine. It's a shame when a young life is snuffed out." He marched out of the building, leaving her with the feeling that he was anything but fine. His shoulders were rigid, his movements sharp with barely contained anger.

At the Misty Hollow campground, they split up; Shea took the campers, while Trevor went to question those in the cabins, including both rental and permanent residents. The campground sprawled along the eastern shore of the lake, a mix of RV sites, tent areas, and small wooden cabins nestled among the trees.

First stop, a small convenience store that sold ice, bait, and anything a camper might have forgotten to bring. The building was weathered cedar with a screen door that squeaked when she pushed it open. A bell above the door announced her arrival.

The clerk, a young man in his early twenties with shoulder-length hair and multiple piercings, welcomed her, his eyes widening at the sight of her uniform. Shea introduced herself. "A body was found this morning on the other side of the lake. I'm wondering whether you might've seen or heard anything."

He shook his head, nervously adjusting his name tag that read 'MIKE.' "I just got here. The store is closed at night. The owner is in the back room. Want me to get him?"

"Please." Shea pasted on a smile, glancing around the cramped store. Shelves lined with canned goods, fishing supplies, and camping necessities created narrow aisles—a handwritten sign advertised night crawlers and minnows.

The boy rushed through a door marked

"EMPLOYEES ONLY," returning a few seconds later with a middle-aged man wiping grease from his hands with a red shop rag. "Can I help you?"

Shea repeated her question.

"I don't know if this is relevant or not, but right before closing, a man wearing a hoodie came in and bought duct tape and cough syrup." The owner, whose name tag identified him as "EARL," scratched his beard thoughtfully.

"Cough syrup? Did you get a good look at his face?"

The man shrugged. "Sorry. He kept his head down. Paid with cash, exact change. Seemed like he wanted to get out of here quick. Thing is, we don't get many folks buying that combination of items, you know? Made me wonder what he was up to."

"What kind of cough syrup?"

"The generic stuff with dextromethorphan. Kids sometimes buy it to get high. This guy had soft hands, like he hadn't worked a hard day his whole life."

Shea thanked him and left the store. Maybe ten sites were occupied by campers. With it being Saturday morning, she expected more to arrive throughout the day. She went from site to site and found out nothing useful. Most campers had retired early, tired from hiking or fishing. By ten, they had extinguished fires and gone to bed. Only one family commented on their dog barking around ten, but they hushed it quickly, not wanting to disturb other campers.

An elderly couple in a pristine RV mentioned seeing a vehicle with only one working headlight driving slowly through the campground around ten-thirty. Still, they couldn't provide any other details.

They had nothing to go on but a man in a hoodie who'd purchased tape and cough syrup. Abby hadn't been killed or bound with either of those items, but the purchases felt significant somehow. Shea went in search of Trevor, following a winding path through the cabin area.

~

Trevor knocked on the door of a small cabin painted forest green with white trim. A woman wearing a frilly white apron decorated with red apples opened the door with a smile. "I wasn't expecting visitors so early."

"I'm Deputy Bolton, ma'am. May I ask you a few questions?" He showed her his ID, noting how her friendly demeanor shifted to concern as she read his badge.

"Absolutely. I'm Mrs. Brown." She pulled the door closed and invited him to have a seat in one of the rockers on her porch. The chairs were well-worn but comfortable, positioned to take advantage of the lake view.

He gazed across the lake, noting how the morning mist had finally lifted, revealing the far shore where they'd found Abby's body. "Beautiful view you've got."

"The primary reason my husband, may he rest in

peace, built this place. Now, what can I do for you?" Her voice carried a slight tremor, the kind that came with age and worry.

"A body was found this morning on the other side of the lake. Do you recall anything out of the ordinary last night, around ten p.m.?"

Her brow furrowed as she rocked slowly, the chair creaking rhythmically. "I did see headlights moving real slow. Thought maybe it was someone looking for a good spot to go night fishing. It happens. The strange thing is, they never turned off their vehicle. Not for a good twenty to thirty minutes, then the vehicle left quicker than it arrived."

"Are you usually awake at that time of night?"

She chuckled, though the sound held little humor. "When you get to be my age, sleep is a luxury not often granted. I sit out here most evenings until sleep beckons. Sometimes that's midnight, sometimes later."

"Did you notice anything else about the vehicle? Size, color, make?"

"Too dark and too far away. But it was definitely larger than a car, a pickup truck, or maybe an SUV. The headlights sat high off the ground, although only one headlight worked."

Seeing Shea approaching along the lake path, Trevor handed the woman a business card. "Thank you for your time, Mrs. Brown. If you remember anything else, please call."

He went to meet Shea halfway, noting the

frustrated set to her shoulders. "Find out anything?"

"Nothing useful. You?"

He told her about the vehicle Mrs. Brown had seen. "No way of knowing the make or model from this distance. We can try to find tire tracks."

She nodded, glancing back toward the convenience store. "Man in a hoodie bought duct tape and cough syrup right before closing. Owner said he kept his head down, had soft hands."

"Doesn't match what we found at the scene, but it's suspicious timing."

"Lead the way."

After studying the area, the older woman had said she'd seen the lights, so he drove them to the other side of the lake. It didn't take long to find a small patch of dirt used for launching boats into the water from trucks. The area was rutted from years of use, with a concrete ramp extending into the lake.

Large tire tracks marred the wet ground. The tread looked like half the ones found in Misty Hollow and surrounding areas—a common pattern that wouldn't narrow their search much.

Trevor approached the water in one direction, while Shea moved in the opposite way, both searching methodically along the shoreline. A sliver of white poked from under a rock near the water's edge. After pulling on a glove, he slipped the paper free. The water smeared the words, but they were still readable. "Shea."

She hurried to his side, her boots squelching in the

mud. "What did you find?"

He handed her the paper, watching her face as she read the message. The words were written in block letters with blue ink, partially dissolved but clear enough to make out.

"She shouldn't have gone out alone after dark."

Chapter Two

Abby's mother answered the front door, still dressed in her robe, her hair disheveled as if she'd been running her fingers through it. Her brow furrowed at the sight of Shea and Trevor standing there in uniform, their expressions grave in the morning light. "Can I help you?"

"May we come in?" Shea hated bringing devastating news to parents. She'd done it too many times in her career, and it never got easier. The Pearson home would never be the same after this conversation.

"Is this about Abby?" Mrs. Pearson clutched the neckline of her robe, her knuckles white against the faded blue terry cloth. Her voice carried the tremor of a mother who already sensed the worst.

"Ma'am, please." Shea motioned at the door, noting how the woman's face had drained of color.

"Deloris?" A man came around the corner of the house, a cigarette dangling from his lips, work clothes stained with motor oil. "What's going on?"

"It's about Abby, Larry." The woman's voice shook, and she wrapped her arms around herself as if trying to hold her world together.

He tossed the cigarette and ground it beneath his steel-toed boot, the ember dying in the damp morning earth. "Come on in then." His shoulders slumped as he led the way inside, his hand finding his wife's elbow in a gesture of support that spoke of years of marriage.

A clean home with old, but well-cared-for furniture filled the front room. The couch showed wear at the arms where hands had rested over the years, and the coffee table bore the ring stains of countless mugs. Photos of Abby in different stages of life adorned the mantel—first steps, school pictures with gap-toothed smiles, dance recitals, and recent senior portraits that captured her shy but genuine smile.

The Pearsons perched on a love seat upholstered in a dark brown fabric, their bodies angled toward each other in unconscious support. Mrs. Pearson's hands twisted a tissue until it fell apart into white shreds.

"Spit it out, Sheriff," Mr. Pearson said, his voice rougher than usual. "Where's our girl?"

Shea cleared her throat, wishing there was an easier way to shatter these people's world. "A body was found this morning at Misty Lake. We need you to come to the morgue in Langley to identify the body."

"Our Abby?" Mrs. Pearson's eyes filled with desperate hope, the kind that clings to impossible odds.

"Can't be. She would've gone home from dance class with one of her friends last night. She always does. There was a recital coming up next month, and they'd been staying late to practice. She was so excited—she had a solo piece this year."

Mr. Pearson took his wife's hand. "Sometimes she went for a hike afterward, remember?"

"Her friend's name?"

"Maggie Spencer. Sweet girl, curly red hair. They've been best friends since middle school." Mrs. Pearson's voice grew stronger as she spoke about the familiar, as if discussing ordinary things could make this moment feel normal too.

"You already know it's Abby, don't you?" Mr. Pearson's weathered face paled, the years of outdoor work suddenly standing out in sharp relief against his ashen skin. "You found her driver's license."

"Yes, sir, and a heart necklace." She showed them a photo on her phone, watching their faces carefully.

The man nodded slowly, his Adam's apple bobbing as he swallowed hard. "We'll head to Langley as soon as my wife is dressed, but Abby didn't own a necklace like that. She wasn't much for jewelry, except for the little pearl earrings her grandmother gave her."

Mrs. Pearson leaned forward, studying the photo more closely. "Where would she have gotten that? It's not her style at all. She preferred simple things, nothing flashy or cheap."

"I'm sorry." Shea swallowed past the boulder in her

throat as Trevor handed the man a business card. "We'll have more questions later this afternoon. Please come into the office after you've identified the body." She gave a grim nod and followed Trevor from the house, leaving the couple to face the worst moment of their lives.

"Where to now?" Trevor asked in the car as he buckled his seatbelt, his movements sharp with suppressed emotion. These family visits always hit him hard.

"The dance studio. The instructor might be the last person, other than the killer, to have seen Abby alive." Shea backed from the Pearsons' driveway, noting the well-tended garden and the basketball hoop over the garage—remnants of a childhood that had ended far too soon. She headed down Main Street, past the familiar storefronts of their small town.

The dance studio sat between the coffee shop and the bookstore in a row of connected buildings that dated back to the 1940s. A black and white striped awning hung over the glass door, which depicted the silhouette of a dancing ballerina in black vinyl. Through the window, Shea spotted mirrors lining the walls and a wooden barre running the length of the room. A bell jingled as they stepped through the door, and the scent of rosin and floor wax filled the air.

A woman in black tights and a sheer flowing skirt greeted them, her hair pulled back in a perfect bun secured with bobby pins. She moved with the fluid grace of someone who'd spent years training her body. "Welcome to Misty Dance. I'm Sierra Valdez. Can I help you?"

"We were told Abby Pearson was a student here?" Shea asked, noting the woman's immediate brightening at the mention of Abby's name.

"Yes." The woman's frown appeared when she registered their uniforms and serious expressions. "Is she in trouble? That doesn't sound like Abby at all."

"Did she attend class yesterday?" Shea chose not to answer the woman's question, watching Sierra's face for any signs of discomfort.

"Of course. Abby never missed. We practice three times a week because we have a recital coming up in just four weeks. Abby was one of my best students— such natural grace, and she worked harder than anyone else." She pointed to a blown-up photo on the wall, pride evident in her voice. The photographer had caught Abby in mid-leap, her face lit with pure joy, arms extended like wings.

"What time did she leave here last night?"

"Nine sharp. We practice from seven to nine on Fridays. I'm very strict about the schedule because most of the girls have curfews." She glanced from Shea to Trevor and back to Shea, worry creeping into her expression. "Please. What is going on? You're scaring me."

"Did she leave with anyone?"

Sierra shook her head, her hands clasping and

unclasping in front of her. "She usually leaves with Maggie Spencer—they carpool most days—but Maggie's grandmother had been taken to the hospital earlier, so she left at eight-thirty to be with her family."

"Do you know of anyone who might want to hurt Abby?"

"Oh, Lord. Something has happened to her." She sagged against the front counter, her dancer's posture crumbling. "Everyone loved Abby. She was quiet, had this way of making people feel comfortable. The younger students adored her; she'd help them with their positions and never got impatient." She took a deep, shuddering breath. "She left out the back door last night instead of the front. I remember because I was locking up and I heard the back door close."

"Is that normal?" Trevor asked, pulling out his notebook.

Sierra shrugged, wiping her eyes with the back of her hand. "It is if the girls aren't waiting for a ride out front. The back door leads to the alley, and there's a shortcut to Maple Street through there. Abby lived on Maple Street."

Shea spotted a camera mounted high in the corner, its red light blinking steadily. "Can we check the security footage?"

"Of course." She led them to a small office crammed with costumes hanging from hooks, competition trophies on every available surface, and a desk covered in registration forms and recital programs.

She booted up a desktop computer that looked like it had seen better days. "We have cameras inside the studio, out front and out back. My insurance company insisted on this after we experienced some vandalism issues last year. Take all the time you need. I have a toddler class beginning in a few minutes." With a deep breath, Sierra straightened her shoulders, pasted on a professional smile, and sailed from the room.

"Why didn't you tell her Abby's dead?" Trevor asked as he navigated to the previous night's camera footage, the old computer running slowly.

"Not until the parents have given a positive ID. Word travels fast in Misty Hollow. Having the news circulate before it's official will only add to the pain for the parents, and it could compromise our investigation." Shea pulled up a chair beside him, noting how his jaw was clenched tight.

The camera in the lobby showed girls leaving in pairs throughout the evening, parents coming and going to pick up their daughters, but no Abby until almost nine. The timestamp showed 8:58 when she appeared, hugging a girl with curly red hair, Maggie, presumably, and waving goodbye to several other students. She moved with that same fluid grace evident in the photograph, even in casual clothes. At 9:01, she stepped out of camera range toward the back of the building.

They switched to the back-alley camera and picked her up again at 9:05. Abby turned right and strolled out of sight, her dance bag slung over her shoulder, seemingly without a care in the world. But to the left, Shea spotted a glint of movement in a window reflection. A figure in a dark hoodie stepped from behind a dumpster, keeping to the shadows. The footage was grainy, but clear enough to see that the hooded figure proceeded in the same direction as Abby, maintaining a careful distance.

"Jerk," Trevor muttered. "He was waiting for her."

"I need to ask the instructor a question. Keep studying the footage. See if you can enhance that image or get a better angle." Shea left the office and entered a studio where eight three- to five-year-olds in pink tutus held onto a barre in front of a mirror that spanned the length of one wall. Their chatter filled the room as they attempted to follow Sierra's patient instructions.

"Excuse me, children. Miss Sierra will be right back." Keeping her smile in place, Sierra stepped out of the room to speak with Shea, closing the door behind her. "Yes? Did you find something?"

"Have you seen anyone new hanging around the studio recently? Someone who showed unusual interest in Abby's group?"

Sierra's eyes widened, her hand flying to her throat. "There was a guy a few days ago—Wednesday, I think. Not a parent, and definitely not someone I recognized from town. Mid-thirties, maybe older. He would stand across the street near the bookstore and watch the girls come and go. When I called out to him, asked if he needed help, he just walked away quickly."

"Can you describe him better?"

"Average height, thin build. He wore a baseball cap pulled low, so I never got a good look at his face. Dark jacket, jeans. The thing that struck me was how he stood so still, just watching. It made my skin crawl."

"You didn't report it to anyone?"

"I thought about calling the police, but he never approached anyone or did anything threatening. I figured he might be a drifter just passing through town. When I didn't see him again, I forgot about it." Her voice carried the guilt of hindsight.

Shea rejoined Trevor in the office. "Anything new on the footage?"

"I've been through it three times. Whoever this is, they knew the camera angles. They stayed in the shadows, kept their head down. But look at this—" He pointed to the screen. "The way they move, the stride length. This could be a woman."

She told him about the stranger who'd been watching the studio. "Let's check the alley."

The narrow alley behind the dance studio reeked of damp garbage and a faint mildew odor. Brick walls rose on either side, creating a canyon of shadows even in daylight. A rusted dumpster, once painted bright blue but now faded and dented, sat halfway down the wall. A storm drain gurgled nearby, and puddles from the previous day's rain reflected the overcast sky.

They scanned the area in methodical silence, looking for anything out of place. Trevor crouched beside the dumpster, his knees popping with the movement. "Footprint in something spilled. Sticky, looks like soda."

Shea joined him, careful not to disturb the evidence. The print was clear in the dried liquid, and it matched the pattern they'd found by the lake. The size was telling—small for a man, but larger than Abby's delicate feet. "We could be looking at a female perpetrator, or maybe a teenage boy."

Trevor snapped several photos with his phone from different angles. "I'll call the crime scene techs to secure the area and make a proper cast of this."

A scrap of dark fabric fluttered from a sharp edge of the dumpster where it had caught and torn. Shea plucked it off using only her fingernails, careful not to contaminate it with her prints. The material felt like a cotton blend, possibly from a hoodie or sweatshirt. "We need to get this to the lab for fiber analysis."

A faint sound reached her ears. The soft scuff of a shoe on concrete. She turned, her hand instinctively moving toward her weapon. "Did you hear that?"

"Hear what?" Trevor straightened, his senses now alert.

The sound came again, closer this time. Footsteps, trying to be quiet but failing on the gritty pavement. "Sounds like someone's trying not to be heard. I don't think we're alone out here."

They moved to opposite ends of the alley, effectively boxing in whoever might be lurking. But after several tense minutes of silence, they found nothing. Whoever had been there was gone, leaving only the lingering feeling of being watched.

Three days later, a vigil was held for Abby at The Misty Hollow Community Church. The building stood at the corner of Main and Church Streets, its stone walls weathered by decades of mountain winters but still imposing against the gray sky. Inside, the sanctuary was hushed with grief. Wooden pews lined the center aisle, their surfaces worn smooth by generations of worshippers. Afternoon light filtered through stained-glass windows depicting biblical scenes in rich blues and golds.

Standing at the carved oak pulpit was Pastor Townsend, relatively new to Misty Hollow after the retirement of the beloved Pastor McKenzie six months earlier. His partially gray hair had been carefully combed to cover a bald spot, and his black suit looked freshly pressed for the solemn occasion.

He placed his weathered hand on the leather-bound Bible and cleared his throat, the sound echoing in the vaulted space. "We are here today to mourn the loss of Abby Pearson. A beloved daughter, devoted student, and gentle soul taken from us at far too young an age. While we grieve this terrible loss, I implore all of you to remain vigilant. Evil walks among us, and we cannot lose any more of our precious children to its darkness."

His words hung heavy in the air, and Shea noticed several parents pulling their children closer to them.

The pastor's sermon was longer than she'd expected, dwelling on themes of protection and the corruption that could lurk beneath the surface of their peaceful community.

After the service, Pastor Townsend and his wife, Marilyn, positioned themselves at the front steps to greet those in attendance as they filed out. Marilyn was a thin woman in her fifties with steel-gray hair pulled back in a severe bun. She wore a black dress that seemed to drain the remaining color from her pale complexion.

She dabbed at her eyes with a white lace handkerchief, though Shea noticed the tears seemed performative rather than genuine. When Mrs. Pearson approached, Marilyn grasped the grieving mother's hands and held them longer than seemed appropriate.

"If you need any help at all once you have Abby's... body back, please let me know. I would consider it an honor to help you plan her memorial service. The church has beautiful arrangements with local florists, and I've organized many such services over the years."

"Thank you," Mrs. Pearson said softly, her voice barely audible. She looked fragile, as if a strong wind might blow her away.

Shea studied each person as they exited the building, cataloging faces and reactions. Everyone seemed genuinely sad at Abby's passing: classmates with red-rimmed eyes, teachers who had known her since elementary school, and neighbors who had watched her grow up. No one seemed to focus too intensely on any of Abby's friends, and the conversations were appropriately subdued.

Marilyn Townsend and Pastor Townsend spent what appeared to be equal amounts of time with each mourner, mere seconds of condolences, except for the extended interaction with the Pearsons.

"Maybe the killer didn't attend," Trevor said quietly, his eyes also scanning the dispersing crowd.

"Oh, he, or she, is here, thriving on the grief filling this place. Killers often attend their victims' services. They want to see the impact of their actions, to feel superior to all these grieving people." She kept a shrewd gaze on the crowd, looking for anyone who seemed too interested, too satisfied, or too detached.

Under a large oak tree at the edge of the churchyard, a young red-haired girl stepped into the embrace of a young man with sandy brown hair. He was tall and lean, probably a high school athlete. They kissed softly, and she leaned her cheek against his chest, seeking comfort in his solid presence.

Marilyn Townsend's expression immediately soured. She frowned deeply, then marched in their direction with purposeful strides, her black heels clicking sharply on the walkway. The young couple pulled apart before she reached them.

Shea couldn't hear what was said, but from the immediate redness that flooded both young people's faces and the way they stepped apart, she figured they'd received a stern lecture about what the pastor's wife perceived as proper behavior at a vigil.

"Harsh." Trevor shook his head, his expression darkening. "That's Maggie Spencer, Abby's best friend. Nothing wrong with seeking comfort from your boyfriend on a day like today. That woman's got ice water in her veins."

"Pastor's wife thought differently. Some people use tragedy as an excuse to impose their moral judgments on others." She turned and headed for the car, noting how Marilyn Townsend continued to glare at the young couple even as they walked away. "I've got a gut feeling, Trevor. Let's head back to the office and dig into the archives. I want to check the past few years for other drowning victims, particularly young women. Any suspicious deaths that might have been ruled accidental."

"You think we've got a serial killer?"

"I think we've got someone who's done this before, yes. That note by the lake, the careful planning, the way he knew to avoid the camera angles—this wasn't his first time. And in a county this small, there should be a pattern if we know where to look."

Chapter Three

Shea stared at files on the computer until the words started to blur together in a haze of dates, names, and forensic details. On the table around her were scattered old autopsy reports, crime scene photos that made her stomach clench, and weather logs going back three years. Her dark-rimmed glasses, still unfamiliar on her face, slid down her nose for the hundredth time that afternoon.

"When did you start wearing glasses?" A steaming cup of coffee in each hand, Trevor stopped a foot into the cramped conference room they'd commandeered for their investigation.

"About a week ago. Need them for the computer work now." She kept her focus on the monitor, scrolling through another case file. "Getting old, I guess." The admission stung more than she cared to admit.

"Sexy." He set a cup near her right hand, the ceramic making a soft clink against the wooden table.

"You're wheezing. Where's your inhaler?"

"Am I?" She frowned, suddenly aware of the tightness in her chest that always came when stress and old injuries combined. She reached into her jacket pocket, pulled out the small blue inhaler, and took a measured puff. The familiar metallic taste filled her mouth. "I have found some girls, all drowned. No concrete evidence yet if their deaths are related, other than they were all found with a heart necklace identical to Abby's. Why didn't anyone make the connection before now?"

"Drownings are, unfortunately, common around bodies of water in a county like ours." Trevor sat heavily at the table and pulled a manila file folder in front of him, the metal chair scraping against the linoleum floor. "Rural areas, lots of lakes and ponds, kids who think they're invincible. Let me hear what you've got."

Shea adjusted her glasses and consulted her handwritten notes. "Millie Phillips, age sixteen. Left the dance studio after evening practice, never made it home. Found the next morning in a rowboat on Crescent Lake. Grace Hutchins, age fifteen. Left choir practice at the Methodist church on Oak Street, found the next morning in a kayak on the bank of Wilson's Pond." She paused, looking up at Trevor. "Both girls looked as if they were sleeping peacefully, hands folded over their chests in a prayer position. Just like Abby Pearson."

Trevor flipped through several pages of crime scene photographs, his jaw tightening with each image. "Someone placed them that way post-mortem. This level of care, this staging—it's not accidental."

"Exactly." Shea nodded, pulling off her glasses to rub her tired eyes. "It's not just the drowning that bothers me. It's the ritual aspect. The staging." She tapped the photo in front of Trevor with her pen. "Look at this—same ligature marks on the back of the neck where each girl was held under the water. The original autopsy reports don't mention ether, but I'm betting it was used in every case, same as with Abby, to subdue the victims until they could be transported to water."

"Very few defensive wounds on any of them," Trevor continued, studying the medical examiner's notes. "These girls knew their attacker, trusted them enough to get close. Or they were incapacitated before they could fight back effectively."

"No sign of extended captivity, no sexual assault, no evidence of recreational drugging." Shea straightened in her chair and crossed her arms, feeling the familiar weight of a complex case settling on her shoulders. "The killer wasn't motivated by the usual things that drive most murders."

Trevor continued reading through the files. "Here are two more cases I pulled from the database. Emily Swanson, seventeen, was found in a fishing boat on Miller's Creek. Angela Phillips—wait, Phillips. Same last name as Millie."

"Sisters?"

"Cousins, according to this. Angela was sixteen, found in a canoe on Bear Lake. That makes five other girls who all died in circumstances nearly identical to Abby Pearson."

"We have a serial killer on our hands, Trevor." Shea's blood chilled as the full scope of what they were dealing with became clear. "Six victims over three years. That's two per year, almost like clockwork."

"Let's think about the motivation here. The care the killer took with each victim, the way they were positioned, the identical necklaces." Trevor stood and walked to the blank whiteboard mounted on one wall of the room. "What does this staging tell us?"

"The killer lost someone. A girl around that age, probably someone very close to them. They're not just staging these victims for shock value—they're replacing someone. Recreating a memory, maybe trying to give that person the peaceful death they didn't have."

"That's an excellent theory." Trevor glanced around for markers. "I think we have enough information to start a proper case board. Visual connections might help us see patterns we're missing."

"Write down all the girls' names chronologically. I'll get photos from the yearbooks Mrs. Patterson dropped off earlier." She pulled several index cards from the stack in the middle of the table and started writing detailed observations. *Victim's hair smoothed and arranged. Eyes closed, mouth shut in peaceful expression—no sign of dirt, blood, or leaves on the body despite outdoor locations. Always left near calm water in a water vessel of some kind. Bodies discovered in the early morning hours by innocent parties.*

Once she finished, she handed the cards to Trevor, who began organizing them on the board with pieces of tape. "The girls don't all have the same hair color or build. The closest thing they have in common is that they're all between fifteen and seventeen years old, and they were all out alone when taken."

"At night, specifically. Don't forget the killer's note about Abby not going out alone after dark." Trevor took a sip of his coffee and grimaced. "Stone cold. There's a small marina about two miles from Misty Lake. Lakeside Rentals—they rent canoes, rowboats, and kayaks. We should check their rental logs going back five years. I know Abby's killer used a boat conveniently left on shore by those boys, but maybe he rented vessels for the others."

"Good thinking. Let's go." Shea stood, gathering the files and sliding them into a manila envelope. "If we don't catch this person soon, another girl is going to die. And based on the timeline, it could be any day now."

On the way to the car, Shea spoke again, her voice thoughtful. "There has to be a deeper connection beyond just age and gender. Something specific these girls had in common. A group they all belonged to, a place they all frequented, someone they all knew and trusted."

"Want to stop at the high school first? Check their activity records?" Trevor slid into the driver's seat, adjusting the rearview mirror.

"It's closer than the marina, and we need those yearbooks anyway." Shea buckled her seatbelt, watching the late afternoon shadows lengthen across Main Street.

They were running against the clock now. If her hunch was correct about a serial killer operating in Misty Hollow, and if the pattern held, they didn't have much time before the next victim was chosen. The killer seemed to operate on a schedule, and summer was when teenage girls were most likely to be out alone in the evenings.

Should she enforce a curfew? That would put fear in the hearts of residents and might drive the killer underground. Call in the FBI? Did they have enough evidence to justify bringing in federal resources, or would the bureaucracy slow them down?

"I can hear your brain spinning from here." Trevor shot her a quick glance as they stopped at the town's only traffic light.

"Trying to figure out my next move. This is bigger than anything we've handled before." She rubbed her temples, where a headache was beginning to build.

He reached over and gave her hand a gentle squeeze. "We'll get this guy. We haven't failed yet, and we're not going to start now."

There was always a first time for failure, and she'd

come close to losing cases more than once in her career. The thought of another young life being lost while the killer remained free made her stomach turn. She forced a smile and pulled her hand free to stare out the window at the familiar streets of her town. Maybe someday, she'd feel completely confident in her abilities as sheriff.

At the high school, they were ushered through corridors lined with student artwork and trophy cases into a small conference room, where they waited for the assistant principal. Shea drummed her fingers on the polished tabletop, studying the motivational posters on the walls. *Reach for the Stars. Your Potential is Limitless.* The irony wasn't lost on her—six young women would never reach their potential now.

She glanced up as a woman in her forties, arms full of yearbooks and thick file folders, entered the room. Her graying hair was pulled back in a practical ponytail, and she wore the slightly harried expression of someone juggling too many responsibilities.

"I'm sorry to keep you waiting. The librarian was busy with checkout, and I had to wait for her to pull these records. I'm Mrs. West, the assistant principal." She placed the yearbooks on the table with a soft thud. "The receptionist said you need me to look up some former students?"

"Deceased students." Shea forced herself to appear more relaxed than she felt. Inside, her nerves were strung as tight as guitar strings, and the coffee wasn't helping. She slid a handwritten list of the drowned victims across the polished table. "We're looking for any connection between these girls."

Mrs. West paled visibly as she read the names. "I wasn't working here when most of these girls died, but I heard about them. Tragic accidents, we were told." She sat across from Shea and Trevor, opening the first file folder. "Let me cross-reference their activities and classes."

After several minutes of flipping through records and comparing entries, she turned to the yearbooks with growing excitement. "They weren't all in the same grade level, and they didn't share the same sports or clubs. But wait—here we go." She turned two of the yearbooks so they could see the group photos. "Different years, so they weren't in the program simultaneously, but all of these girls, including Abby Pearson, were participants in our Peer Mentor Program."

Trevor leaned closer to examine the photographs. "Who's the adult supervisor in these photos?"

"That's Roger Watson, one of our English teachers. He came to us right out of college about six years ago. The students loved him—he had this way of connecting with them, especially the ones who were struggling." Her voice carried genuine fondness.

"You speak of him in the past tense," Shea observed, her detective instincts sharpening.

"Roger no longer teaches here. He, uh," she cleared

her throat uncomfortably, "became romantically involved with one of our seniors last year and was terminated. Violation of professional conduct policies. He still lives in Misty Hollow, though. Works as a freelance editor now." She pulled a smartphone from her jacket pocket. "He used to maintain a blog about literature and local history. There hasn't been anything new posted since this photo went up last year." She handed Shea the phone.

The screen displayed a haunting photograph of a teenage girl lying peacefully in a canoe, her arms folded across her chest, her eyes closed as if she were sleeping. The image was artistic, almost reverent in its composition. Written underneath in elegant script was: *In Loving Memory of Carol Watson, taken too soon by the waters she loved.*

Shea felt her breath catch as she slid the phone to Trevor. The staging was nearly identical to their crime scenes.

Trevor's features hardened as he studied the image. "I think we just found our primary suspect. When did his sister die?"

Mrs. West consulted another file. "According to his employment records, he requested bereavement leave five years ago for his sister's drowning. Carol was sixteen."

"Thank you for your time and cooperation." Shea stood abruptly, her mind racing. Outside in the hallway, she called the office. "Doris, I need you to pull everything you can find on Roger Watson—address, vehicle registration, criminal history, everything."

"I've met Roger socially," Trevor said as they walked quickly toward the exit. "Quiet, unassuming man. Reads a lot, keeps to himself. Honestly, it doesn't strike me as a killer."

"That's exactly what people said about Ted Bundy." Shea pushed through the glass doors into the late afternoon sunshine. "Charming, educated, seemed harmless. It's often the ones who blend in perfectly that are the most dangerous."

Roger Watson lived in a modest one-story red brick house on Elm Street, nestled between towering pine trees that cast long shadows across the well-maintained lawn. The property was immaculate but unremarkable—precisely the kind of place where a serial killer could hide in plain sight. A small garden of white roses bordered the front walkway, and Shea noticed they were the same variety that had been placed on Abby's makeshift altar.

Trevor knocked sharply on the dark green front door. After several moments, they heard footsteps approaching, and the door opened to reveal Watson, a thin man in his early thirties with wire-rimmed glasses that kept sliding down his nose. He wore a gray cardigan sweater, despite the warm weather, and had a pale, almost translucent complexion, indicating that he spent most of his time indoors.

"Sheriff Callahan. Deputy Bolton." He blinked

owlishly at them, clearly surprised by their presence. His hands trembled slightly as he adjusted his glasses. "Something I can do for you?"

"We'd like to ask you a few questions, Roger." Trevor's voice carried a subtle coolness.

"Of course. Please, come in." Roger stepped back to allow them entry, his movements nervous and bird-like. "Excuse the mess. I wasn't expecting company."

The living room was exactly what Shea expected from an English teacher: floor-to-ceiling bookshelves lined one entire wall, filled with classic literature, poetry collections, and writing guides. She noticed several books about grief and loss prominently displayed. A cold cup of coffee sat forgotten next to a laptop on the dining table, and a bestselling mystery novel lay open on an end table, a bookmark protruding from about halfway through. What caught her attention, though, were the framed photographs scattered throughout the room—all of the same young woman at various ages.

"Your sister?" Shea asked, gesturing toward the photos.

"Yes, Carol." His voice immediately softened with affection and a hint of pain. "She would have been twenty-one this year."

"You used to run the Peer Mentor Program at the high school?" Trevor asked, settling onto a worn leather couch that had seen better days.

"Yes, I did. I started that program about four years

ago in hopes of addressing some of the bullying issues we were seeing among students. Peer support can be incredibly effective. Young people often relate better to someone closer to their age." His eyes lit up as he discussed the program, his passion evident despite his obvious discomfort with their visit. "The girls especially seemed to benefit. They were dealing with so much pressure, academic stress, social media, and body image issues. Why do you ask?"

"Are you aware of the recent death of Abby Pearson?" Shea remained standing, preferring the psychological advantage of height during interrogations.

"I heard about it, certainly. Tragedy." He sat heavily in a wingback chair across from Trevor, his hands clasping and unclasping nervously. "But I didn't know the girl personally. She would have been in the program after I left the school. Though I do remember seeing her at the dance studio sometimes when I picked up coffee from next door."

"Tell us about the circumstances of your leaving the school," Shea said, overseeing his body language.

Roger's face flushed red. "I... I made a serious error in judgment. I became involved with a student named Sarah Mitchell. She was eighteen, a senior, but it was completely inappropriate and unprofessional. I lost my teaching license, my career, everything." He removed his glasses and cleaned them with shaking hands. "It was the worst mistake of my life."

"How did that relationship start?" Trevor pressed.

"Sarah was struggling with depression after her grandmother died. She stayed after school frequently to talk, and I... I let my professional boundaries slip. She reminded me so much of Carol, the same gentle spirit, the same way of looking at the world." His voice grew quieter. "I know how that sounds, but it wasn't about her age. It was about filling the hole that Carol's death left in my life."

"What about this?" Shea showed him the screenshot of his blog post, watching his face for any reaction.

Pain flickered across his eyes like a physical blow, and his shoulders sagged. "That's my sister Carol. She drowned when she was sixteen, five years ago this summer." His voice cracked as he continued. "She took our father's old canoe out alone that day. I begged her not to go. The weather was turning stormy, and she wasn't a strong swimmer. But Carol was always stubborn, always thought she knew better than everyone else."

"Can you tell us more about what happened that day?" Shea asked gently, noting how his hands trembled as he spoke.

"It was a Saturday in July. Carol had been upset about something—she wouldn't tell me what, but she'd been crying earlier that morning. She said she needed to think, needed to be alone on the water." Roger stood and walked to the window, staring out at his garden. "I found her body the next morning. She was... peaceful. Just like she was sleeping, floating in that damn canoe."

"Who else knew about Carol's death? Did you ever share details with your students?" Trevor asked.

"Only in general terms. Sometimes when students were dealing with loss, I'd mention that I understood their pain because I'd lost my sister. But I never showed them that photograph or discussed the specifics." Roger turned back to face them. "Why are you asking all this?"

"We've discovered that several girls who participated in your mentor program have all died in circumstances very similar to how your sister died," Shea said, studying his reaction.

Roger's face went white, and he gripped the back of his chair for support. "What do you mean, similar circumstances?"

"All found in boats or near water, positioned peacefully, hands folded. All drowned, all teenagers." Trevor leaned forward. "And all wearing identical heart necklaces."

"That's... that's impossible. Carol wasn't wearing any necklace when we found her." Roger sank back into his chair, looking genuinely shaken. "You can't think I had anything to do with these girls' deaths. I loved those kids. They were like the little sisters I could never protect."

"Where were you last Friday night between nine and eleven PM?" Shea asked.

"Here, working on a manuscript. I'm editing a romance novel for a client in Chicago. I can show you the email timestamps if you need them." His voice was steadier now, more focused. "Sheriff, I may have made terrible mistakes in my personal life, but I would never hurt any of those girls. They reminded me too much of Carol."

"Tell us about Marilyn Townsend," Trevor said, changing direction. "You mentioned we should speak with her."

Roger's expression darkened slightly. "Marilyn took over the program after I left, but she changed it significantly. Where I focused on academic support and peer counseling, she made it much more... spiritual. Prayer circles, Bible study, and discussions about purity and moral guidance. Some of the girls seemed uncomfortable with the new direction."

"Did any of them complain to you about it?"

"A few reached out after I left the school. They said Marilyn was very intense, very controlling about their personal lives. She had strong opinions about how teenage girls should behave, what activities were appropriate." Roger hesitated. "One girl, I think it was Millie Phillips, said Marilyn made her feel guilty about everything from her clothing choices to spending time with boys."

"Millie Phillips was one of the drowning victims," Shea said quietly.

Roger's face crumpled. "Oh God. I should have

done something, should have reported my concerns to the school administration. But I was already in disgrace. Who would have listened to me?"

"Is there anything else about Marilyn or the program that seemed off to you?" Trevor pressed.

"She was obsessed with the idea of protecting these girls from corruption. She talked constantly about keeping them pure, keeping them safe from the evils of the world." Roger rubbed his temples. "And she asked very detailed questions about my sister's death when she first took over. I wanted to know exactly how it happened, what she was wearing, and how we found her. Said she wanted to understand what grief looked like so she could help the students better."

Shea and Trevor exchanged meaningful glances. "Roger, this is very important. Did you ever show Marilyn that photograph of your sister?"

"Yes, actually. She said it was beautiful, that it captured Carol's peaceful spirit. She asked if she could see it again sometime, said it helped her understand how to honor the memory of lost loved ones." Roger's eyes widened as the implications hit him. "You don't think... You can't think Marilyn is involved in this."

"We're exploring all possibilities," Shea said carefully. "Roger, I need to ask again. Don't leave town for the next few days. And if you remember anything else about your conversations with Marilyn, anything at all, call us immediately."

Roger nodded numbly. "Am I a suspect in

something?"

"Everyone's a suspect until we determine otherwise," Trevor said, standing to leave. "But right now, we're more interested in what you might know than what you might have done."

As they walked back to their car, Shea turned to Trevor. "What do you think?"

"I think Roger Watson is a broken man who made some terrible choices, but I don't think he's our killer. His grief over his sister seems genuine, and his shock at learning about the other deaths felt real."

"Agreed. But he may have inadvertently given our killer the template for these murders. That photograph, the details about how Carol died…if Marilyn Townsend saw that as some blueprint..." Shea shook her head grimly. "We need to dig deeper into the Townsends' background, and we need to do it fast."

"That's where I'm headed." Trevor started the engine and pulled away from the curb.

The parsonage sat directly behind Misty Hollow Community Church, connected by a stone walkway lined with carefully tended flowerbeds. It was a two-story white Victorian with black shutters and a wraparound porch, evoking traditional values and a conservative lifestyle.

Marilyn Townsend knelt in the front garden when they arrived, a wide-brimmed floppy hat protecting her from the late afternoon sun. She straightened from pulling weeds as their patrol car crunched up the gravel driveway, brushing dirt from her gardening gloves.

"Hello there!" A bright smile graced her weathered face, though something in her eyes remained watchful. "This is an unexpected pleasure. Beautiful evening for a visit."

Trevor shot Shea an amused look at the woman's enthusiasm. "Mrs. Townsend, we'd like to ask you some questions about the Peer Mentor Program you run through the church."

"Of course, of course! Always happy to talk about the work we do with young people." She peeled off her gardening gloves and hung them on a hook beside the front door. "Please, come inside. Would you like some sweet tea? I made a fresh pitcher this morning."

"That would be wonderful," Shea said, suddenly realizing how parched she was. "I'm dying of thirst," she whispered to Trevor as they followed Marilyn up the porch steps.

The interior of the house hit them with an overwhelming wave of lavender scent—potpourri, candles, and sachets creating an almost suffocating floral atmosphere. "Have a seat wherever you're comfortable. I'll be right back with refreshments."

"She doesn't seem the least bit upset to see law enforcement at her door," Trevor observed, settling onto a sofa that was drowning in decorative throw pillows of every size and pattern imaginable.

"Why should she be? As far as she knows, we're here for a routine inquiry about the program." Shea shifted beside him, trying to find a comfortable position among the pillow fortress. "I never did understand why some people need so many decorative pillows. You can't use the furniture."

Marilyn returned with a silver tray bearing tall glasses of sweet tea, a crystal bowl filled with sugar cubes, and a plate of perfectly arranged lemon cookies that looked like they belonged in a magazine. She settled into a wingback chair across from them, her posture perfect and her smile never wavering.

"Now then, what can I help you with regarding our mentoring program?"

"How long have you been overseeing it?" Trevor asked, declining the offer of additional sugar for his already-sweet tea.

"About eighteen months now. I took over right after Mr. Watson's... departure from the school district. I love working with young ladies. It gives them something meaningful and purposeful to do while keeping them focused on positive activities." Her enthusiasm seemed genuine, but Shea noticed how her hands moved restlessly, straightening imaginary wrinkles in her skirt.

"Did you know Abby Pearson personally?" Shea asked, dropping three sugar cubes into her glass and stirring slowly.

"Oh yes, such a sweet, gentle girl. Quiet, but with real depth to her character. So horrible what happened to her." Marilyn's fingers found the fringe on a crocheted throw blanket and began worrying it nervously. "I simply cannot understand how such tragedies keep happening in our peaceful community."

Trevor consulted his notes and began reading the names of the other drowning victims from the past three years.

"They all drowned? Like poor Abby?" Marilyn's hand stilled completely, and for just a moment, her composed mask slipped. "I... I hadn't realized there was a pattern. How terrible."

"Was anyone else regularly involved in running the program besides yourself?" Trevor studied the woman's face intently. She seemed concerned and shocked in all the appropriate ways, except for her eyes. They remained calculating, almost cold.

Marilyn shook her head. "It's just me during our regular meetings. Sometimes my husband pops in to say hello to the girls. He's wonderful with young people. The church groundskeeper is around quite a bit during our sessions, but he's never intrusive. Although..." She paused, frowning thoughtfully. "I have noticed him watching the girls as they arrive and leave. Nothing inappropriate, mind you, but he does seem to pay attention to their schedules."

"No one else lives here on the church property besides you and your husband?" Shea asked, glancing around the immaculate living room.

"Just the two of us in the parsonage. Why do you ask?"

"There's a photograph in your dining room, a single portrait of a teenage girl. She looks to be about sixteen." Shea's gaze shifted toward the adjacent room where the framed photo was visible on the wall.

Something flickered across Marilyn's face: pain, guilt, fear, or perhaps all three. "That's our daughter Bella. She died five years ago this summer." The composed mask cracked slightly, revealing genuine anguish beneath.

Trevor leaned forward, his detective instincts sharpening. "She wouldn't have drowned, would she, Mrs. Townsend?"

"How did you know?" Marilyn's voice trembled for the first time since they'd arrived, and her carefully maintained composure finally began to crumble.

"Call it professional intuition. I'm very sorry for your loss, ma'am." He stood, signaling the end of the interview. "Please call us immediately if you think of anything that might help our investigation. Oh, and we'll need the name and contact information for your groundskeeper. And a complete list of all the girls currently participating in the mentoring program."

"That information is confidential. These families trust us with their daughters' privacy."

"We can obtain a warrant if necessary," Shea said firmly, also rising from her seat.

Shoulders slumping in defeat, Marilyn walked to a small desk and wrote out a list of seven names in her careful handwriting. "These are good girls from good families. They don't need you frightening them with aggressive questioning."

"Investigating multiple murders is not aggressive questioning, ma'am. It's our job." Trevor shook his head. "We'll be in touch."

Back in the patrol car, Shea turned to face Trevor before he started the engine. "She was remarkably calm throughout that entire interview. Almost unnaturally controlled."

"Too calm. She's a good actress, but we saw through the performance. Marilyn Townsend knows something significant about these deaths, and I'm willing to bet it's a lot more than she's letting on." Trevor started the car and pulled away from the parsonage. "Question is—is she covering for someone else, or is she more directly involved than we realized?"

53

Chapter Four

The townspeople gathered on the banks of Misty Lake as the sun began its slow descent toward the horizon, painting the sky in muted oranges and purples that reflected off the water's surface. Paper lanterns with flickering candles floated across the placid water like fallen stars, each one carrying a whispered prayer for Abby's soul. Next to the shore, someone had erected a makeshift altar adorned with flowers, stuffed animals, and photos of Abby throughout her short life—school pictures, dance recital shots, candid moments with friends.

Shea stood at the rear of the crowd, her German Shepherd, Heidi, sitting alert at her side. The dog's ears were pricked forward, sensing the tension that rippled through the gathering like invisible waves. Abby's parents clung to each other near the front, Mrs. Pearson's shoulders shook with silent sobs while her husband stood like a statue, his jaw clenched against his grief. Teenagers wept as they placed more flowers at the altar, roses, daisies, baby's breath that Abby had loved from her mother's garden. A low fog crept over the lake, as if nature itself was mourning the loss of someone so young.

Pastor Mark Townsend stepped forward to lead the memorial, his tall frame imposing against the darkening sky. While his words eloquently spoke of how special Abby had been to the community, how her gentle spirit had touched so many lives, his tone somehow lacked the warmth such sentiments should convey. He avoided making eye contact with the gathered mourners, instead seeming to focus on something in the distance beyond the lake. His delivery felt rehearsed, professional rather than personal.

Marilyn remained seated in a folding chair someone had provided, her hands clasped tightly in her lap, knuckles white with tension. Her gaze never wavered from the altar, but her features remained eerily composed—no tears, no visible emotion, just an almost mask-like stillness that unsettled Shea. For a woman who claimed to care deeply about these girls, she showed remarkably little grief.

After the forty-minute service concluded with a hymn that echoed hauntingly across the water, the townspeople naturally gathered in small, hushed groups to share memories and offer comfort to one another. But rather than mingling and offering condolences as they typically did after church services, the Townsends headed at a brisk pace toward their dark sedan, clearly eager to escape the crowd.

"Word around town is that Marilyn shut down the peer mentor program indefinitely," Trevor said, joining Shea near the back of the dispersing crowd.

"Really?" Shea dragged her gaze away from the retreating car, watching as it disappeared around the bend toward the church. "Did anyone say why?"

He shrugged, adjusting his jacket against the evening chill. "Officially, out of respect for the victims. She told several parents that she'd consider restarting it after a proper period of mourning has passed. Maybe in the fall."

"She didn't seem to be doing much mourning tonight. I could've made ice cubes off the frigid air surrounding that woman." Shea watched the last of the paper lanterns drift toward the far shore. "I think it would be worth our time to do some serious digging into the pastor and his wife's background. Find out where they came from, what they left behind."

"You want to start tonight? I can meet you at the office after I grab some dinner."

"No, morning is fine. We both need some rest. This case is starting to wear on us, me at least." She flashed him a tired smile and opened the door of her truck so Heidi could jump into the passenger seat. "Let's make a quick stop at the office to grab those files, then head home and crash in front of the TV. What do you say, girl? It's been a hell of a long day."

Heidi woofed softly in agreement and settled herself to stare out the front windshield, always alert for anything unusual.

In her office, Shea immediately spotted a large manila envelope on her desk that hadn't been there when she'd left for the memorial service. The envelope was unmarked except for her name written in block letters across the front. Frowning, she carefully opened it, using a letter opener rather than her fingers. A Polaroid photograph slipped out and fluttered onto the desktop.

The image showed tonight's vigil from an elevated angle, capturing the entire crowd gathered around the altar. Shea was visible at the back of the group, Heidi at her side. Someone had circled her figure with a red marker, the circle drawn with aggressive, jagged strokes. On a separate sheet of white paper, someone had typed in all capital letters: "STOP INVESTIGATING OR YOU'LL BE THE NEXT ONE FLOATING IN THE LAKE."

Shea's blood ran cold as she realized the implications of what she had just read. Someone had not only attended the memorial service but had managed to take this photo, develop it, and deliver it to her office while she was still at the lake. Since Doris had already gone home for the day, and the building should have been locked, she'd have to wait until morning to ask whether anyone had seen who delivered the threat.

"Come on, girl. Let's get out of here." Shea grabbed the victim files from her desk drawer and headed for the door, suddenly feeling exposed and vulnerable in the empty building. But when she reached her truck in the parking lot, she stopped short and cursed under her breath. All four tires had been slashed, clean cuts that left them completely flat. "You have got to be kidding me."

She glanced up at the parking lot security camera, noting its red recording light was still blinking. "Back inside, Heidi. I need to call for tire service and review tonight's footage." She hadn't been in the building for more than ten minutes. This killer was not only organized but incredibly bold.

After making a quick call to Jim's 24-Hour Auto Service, Shea booted up her computer and pulled up the security camera footage from the past hour. She fast-forwarded through most of it, then paused when a figure in a dark hoodie approached her truck at 8:47 PM—just twelve minutes after she'd entered the building.

The person moved with purpose but seemed deliberately bulky, as if they were wearing extra clothing to disguise their actual body shape and size. From what she could tell, they weren't huge, maybe five-foot-six or so, with a slight build beneath the padding. Could be a teenager, possibly even one of the high school students. It wouldn't be the first time in criminal history that a teen had become a serial killer.

Trevor's brother had been only sixteen when he'd started his killing spree.

Her phone buzzed with a text from Jim, the mechanic, saying he'd already replaced her tires and she could stop by the garage to settle the bill in the morning. As she gathered her things to leave, her gaze fell on her inbox, where another envelope waited among the day's mail and interdepartmental memos. This one had a return address she recognized: Eli Watson.

Shea slipped the letter into one of the victim files and made sure to lock her office door as she left— something she didn't usually bother with, but she didn't want any more unpleasant surprises when she arrived for work in the morning.

At home, she poured herself a generous glass of red wine, fed Heidi her evening meal, and settled into her favorite armchair to read Eli's letter. The handwriting was careful and precise, like someone who'd taken time to organize his thoughts.

Sheriff Callahan,

I hope I haven't overstepped any boundaries by writing to you, but I've done some discreet questioning around town about Marilyn and Mark Townsend. What I discovered might be relevant to your investigation.

Before coming to Misty Hollow, Mark pastored a small country church up around Hickory Hollow about seven years ago. Marilyn ran a very similar youth mentoring program for teenage girls up there through their church. According to my source, a woman who used to attend that church when a sixteen-year-old girl named Rebecca Mills drowned in suspicious circumstances, the Townsends packed up and left town within two weeks, claiming they felt called to minister elsewhere.

But here's what's interesting: two years before the Mills girl's drowning, the Townsends' daughter Bella died—officially ruled an accidental drowning after she fell from a boat on Pine Lake. However, my informant said Bella wasn't supposed to be anywhere near the water that day. She'd told her parents she was going horseback riding with friends and would be home by dinner.

I know I could have called you with this information, but I didn't want to risk anyone overhearing our conversation. Maybe I'm being paranoid, but ever since your visit the other day, I've had the distinct feeling that someone is watching me. I've noticed the same car parked across from my house on two different occasions, and yesterday I'm certain I saw someone duck behind the trees in my backyard when I looked out the kitchen window.

I hope this information helps your investigation. Please be careful. I have a bad feeling about how dangerous this situation is becoming.

Sincerely,
Eli Watson

Shea read the letter twice, her mind racing with the implications. She'd known from questioning the Townsends that their daughter Bella had drowned five years ago, but she hadn't realized there had been another suspicious drowning at their previous church. The pattern was becoming clearer, and it wasn't encouraging.

She pulled out the list of girls currently enrolled in Marilyn's program and spread it across her coffee table. Seven names, seven potential victims if her theory was correct. Tomorrow, she'd have to make time to visit each of these families personally—this was too important to delegate to her deputies. Her instincts were screaming that time was running out for another girl on this list.

The next morning, Shea arrived at the sheriff's office to find the place in complete chaos. Doris rushed toward her before she'd even made it through the front door, her usually perfect hair disheveled and her face pale with stress.

"Sheriff, thank God you're here! Someone broke into the building last night. They seemed particularly focused on your office. They barely touched anything else."

Jaw clenched with anger, Shea strode down the hallway toward her office, Heidi trotting at her heels. The door stood ajar, and she could see the destruction before she even stepped inside. A single glass of water sat prominently in the center of her desk, placed there with obvious intent. Everything that had once been organized on top of the desk, files, reports, office supplies, her coffee mug, now lay scattered across the floor in deliberate chaos.

"Subtle," Trevor said dryly, appearing in the doorway behind her. He crossed his arms and leaned against the doorjamb, surveying the mess. "Someone's definitely trying to send you a message. I take it the water is meant as a drowning threat?"

"Appears that way. I was already sent a note last night telling me to stop investigating or I'd become the next victim floating in the lake." She began methodically picking up papers from the floor, checking each one to make sure nothing was missing. "And just to make their point extra clear, they slashed all four of my tires while I was reviewing the threat."

Trevor immediately dropped to his knees to help her gather the scattered documents. "Why l didn't you call me? I would have come right over."

"What could you have done? The damage was already finished, and Jim had my truck fixed within an hour." She started organizing the recovered papers into neat stacks. "Besides, I needed time to think about what Roger Watson told me in this letter."

She handed him Roger's letter and watched his expression grow increasingly grim as he read. " This case is escalating rapidly, and now you're being directly threatened. Can you promise me you won't investigate anything else without backup?"

"I can promise to try my best. But if something urgent comes up and needs immediate attention, I'm going to handle it." She finished organizing the papers and placed them in secure stacks on her desk. "Starting today, I want to interview each of the girls in Marilyn's program personally. Get a sense of their routines, their safety awareness, maybe identify which one might be most vulnerable."

"Sheriff?" Deputy Butler's voice called from down the hallway before he appeared in her doorway, his face flushed from running. "We've got an emergency call about a teenage girl who didn't make it home last night. Parents are frantic."

Trevor's face fell. "Has anyone started searching the lake yet?"

"Search and rescue teams are mobilizing now, headed out there within the next ten minutes."

"We'll be right behind them." Shea dropped the papers she'd been organizing and motioned for Heidi to follow. She grabbed her jacket and keys, already heading for the door. "What's the missing girl's name?"

"Emily Snopes. Seventeen years old, a junior in high school. Last seen around eight o'clock last night at the town playground."

"That name isn't on Marilyn's list of current program participants," Trevor observed as they hurried toward their patrol cars in the parking lot.

"Which means the killer might be expanding

beyond the mentoring program now. That's going to make it infinitely harder for us to keep this town's teenagers safe." Shea slammed her car door and started the engine. "We can't possibly watch every girl between the ages of fifteen and seventeen."

Trevor turned on his siren and led the way toward Misty Lake, both vehicles racing through the quiet morning streets. The sound echoed off the buildings, alerting the entire town that another crisis was unfolding.

When they arrived at the lake, it was already swarming with concerned townspeople conducting their searches. Someone had brought a drone and was systematically flying it over the water, while others walked the shoreline, calling Emily's name. If Emily had been brought here, any physical evidence would likely have been trampled under the feet of well-meaning volunteers.

"Sheriff!" A girl who looked to be about twelve years old broke away from a family camping area and ran toward Shea, her face urgent with important information. "I saw Emily last night!"

"Where did you see her, sweetheart?" Shea knelt to the girl's eye level, making her feel safe and vital.

The girl pointed toward a small playground about two hundred yards from the main beach area. "She was sitting on one of the swings by herself around eight-thirty. She looked really sad, like she'd been crying."

An older teenage boy, presumably her brother,

jogged over and took the child's hand protectively. "Sophie, you can't just run off like that. Mom and Dad said it's not safe to wander around alone right now."

"But I had to tell them about Emily!" Sophie yanked her hand free from her brother's grip, clearly frustrated by adult rules when she had crucial information to share. "We're camped right over there in the blue tent."

"How can you be sure it was Emily you saw?" Trevor asked gently, pulling out his notebook to record her statement.

"Because I talked to her for a couple of minutes before my parents made me come back to camp. She told me she was waiting for someone, but she seemed nervous about it. I got in trouble because I didn't return before dark like I was supposed to." Sophie didn't look the least bit remorseful about breaking her parents' rules.

"You did exactly the right thing by telling us, Sophie. You've been a tremendous help to our investigation." Shea smiled, then nodded for her brother to escort her back to their family's campsite.

"Sheriff! We've got something." The man operating the search drone shouted from further down the walking path, his voice carrying urgency and dread. "Not in the lake this time. Down by Wilson Creek!"

Trevor shot Shea a meaningful glance, then sprinted in the direction the man was pointing. Shea and Heidi followed close behind, her heart pounding with the terrible certainty of what they were about to find.

The body of a teenage girl lay beside the creek in a small clearing, partially hidden by overhanging willow branches. Her long brown hair was splayed around her head like a dark halo, and her hands were folded peacefully across her stomach in the same ritualistic pose they'd seen with all the other victims. But this time, there was no boat or water vessel; just the muddy creek bank, which showed clear signs of a violent struggle. Emily had fought back hard while being held under the shallow water, her heels digging furrows in the soft earth.

"I want the entire area around this lake completely shut down," Shea ordered, her voice carrying the authority of someone who'd reached the end of her patience. "Campgrounds, rental cabins, picnic areas, hiking trails—everything. I'll set up a schedule for regular patrol coverage. We are going to stop this killer even if I have to declare martial law and shut down the whole town."

As the crime scene team began their careful documentation of Emily's body and the surrounding area, Trevor spotted a man in dirty coveralls standing at the edge of the tree line about fifty yards away. The man watched the proceedings with obvious interest, but tried to remain inconspicuous.

"Isn't that Frank Wilson, the church groundskeeper who also does maintenance work at the high school?" Trevor asked, squinting to get a better look at the distant figure.

With a startled glance toward Shea and Trevor, realizing he'd been noticed, the man suddenly bolted into the thick woods, crashing through underbrush in his haste to escape.

"Well, that's not suspicious at all," Shea muttered grimly. "Looks like we'll be paying Mr. Wilson a very detailed visit first thing tomorrow morning. While it's not particularly strange that he attended last night's vigil, half the town was there. It's suspicious for him to run like a guilty man the moment he realizes we've seen him."

As they watched the groundskeeper disappear deeper into the forest, Shea couldn't shake the feeling that they were finally close to catching their killer. The question was whether they could identify and stop him before another innocent girl paid the ultimate price for his twisted obsession with recreating his lost daughter's death.

Chapter Five

Frank Wilson, the groundskeeper for both the church and the high school, lived in a small, weather-beaten white house at the very edge of the school property. Paint peeled around the window frames, and the front yard was dominated by a rusted pickup truck that looked like it hadn't run in years. Wariness shone from his bloodshot eyes when he opened the door to Trevor's persistent knocking. The odor of alcohol wafted from his breath despite the early hour.

"Sheriff. Deputy." His voice was gravelly, like someone who'd been smoking for decades. "I'm on my way to work." He scratched at his graying beard, leaving flakes of dandruff on his stained work shirt.

"We won't take up much of your time, Mr. Wilson." Shea glanced at the open door, noting how he blocked the entrance with his body.

"Fine." He gave a reluctant wave of his arm, stepping aside to let them into a house that reeked of pipe tobacco, stale beer, and something else, something sour and unpleasant. The interior was cluttered with the accumulation of years of solitary living. Shelves held coffee cans full of nails, rusted tools, yellowed newspapers stacked three feet high, and empty beer bottles…everything but books. A cuckoo clock sounded the hour from somewhere in the depths of the house, its mechanical cry echoing off the cluttered walls. The man crossed his arms defensively over his chest. "Out with it. Like I said, I'm on my way to work."

"Why did you run from the crime scene yesterday, Mr. Wilson?" Shea kept her tone conversational, giving a slight tilt to her head as she did her best to appear non-threatening, despite the tension building in her neck and shoulders.

"I realized I left my crockpot plugged in." The man grinned, revealing several missing teeth and others stained brown from tobacco. "Didn't want to burn the house down, you understand."

Trevor pulled out his notebook, making a show of writing down the excuse. "That's interesting, because we didn't see you leave in the direction of your house. You headed deeper into the woods."

Frank's grin faltered slightly. "Must've gotten turned around. Woods all look the same when you're in a hurry."

"Someone told us you seem overly interested in the girls who belong to the peer mentorship program at the church," Trevor continued, his tone becoming more pointed.

"Ain't true. I keep to myself. Don't bother anyone." Frank's hands clenched into fists at his sides. "People talk too much in this town, make up stories where there ain't any."

"Have you ever taken a stroll around Misty Lake at night?" Shea asked, noting how his left eye twitched when she mentioned the lake.

"Yep. Get insomnia a couple of times a week. Walking clears my head, helps me think." He shrugged. "That ain't a crime, last I heard. Man's got a right to walk on public property."

"No, sir, it isn't a crime." Shea forced a slight smile, though her instincts were screaming that something was off about this man. "During these walks, have you ever seen any of the girls from the program out there?"

"Nope. Like I said, I mind my own business." But his voice had a defensive edge now, and he wouldn't meet her eyes directly.

"Where were you around ten p.m. on Friday night, the night Abby Pearson was murdered?" Shea's gaze fell on the fresh scratches marring his forearm, deep gouges that looked like fingernails had made them. "Those look painful."

Frank instinctively pulled his sleeve down to cover the marks. "I don't rightly recall where I was. Could've been asleep, watching TV, or out walking. Nights all blur together when you live alone."

"How did you get those scratches?" Shea pressed, stepping closer.

"Working. Trimming bushes around the church property. Thorns are vicious this time of year." His face darkened with suspicion and anger. "Are you saying I had something to do with that girl's death? Because if you are, then stop beating around the bush and come out and say it. I got rights, you know."

"We aren't accusing you of anything, Mr. Wilson. We're just trying to get a complete picture of what happened that night." Shea stepped back, recognizing that pushing further without concrete evidence would only make him more defensive. "Have a good day at work."

Without more evidence, they couldn't hold the man or search his property. He didn't have a solid alibi for the night in question, but unfortunately, most of the people they'd spoken with didn't either. As they walked back to their patrol car, Shea noticed curtains twitching in several neighboring houses. Word would spread quickly that the sheriff had been questioning Frank Wilson.

"The school next?" Trevor asked, glancing over the hood of their car at Frank's house, where the man stood in his doorway watching them leave.

"Yes. The principal said we could use the conference room to interview the girls from Marilyn's program." Shea started the engine, feeling the weight of frustration settling on her shoulders. "We need a breakthrough, Trevor. We're no closer to solving these murders than we were the day Abby's body was found."

At Misty Hollow High School, they set up in the same conference room where they'd first learned about the connection between the victims. The principal had arranged for the girls to be excused from classes one at a time, and Shea hoped their youth might make them more forthcoming than the adults they'd been questioning.

The first girl, Madison, was clearly nervous but had little to offer beyond confirming that Abby had seemed upset about something in the weeks before her death. The second girl they spoke to, Kayla, a junior with bright red hair and multiple ear piercings, proved more talkative.

"Abby told me she was planning on not attending any more of the meetings," Kayla said, fidgeting with her cell phone on the conference table. "She said the rules were getting too strict, and she felt like she couldn't be herself anymore."

"Can you expand on that?" Shea leaned forward, sensing this was important. "What kind of rules?"

"Well, it's like Marilyn was trying to be our mom or something, you know?" Kayla made exaggerated finger quotes around the word "mom." "We have this whole list of things we shouldn't do. Can't wear certain clothes, can't listen to certain music, can't hang out with boys unless it's in a group setting. Some of us are no longer seeing the purpose of the program. We hardly ever mentor anyone younger. Mostly, we sit around while Marilyn lectures us about moral behavior."

Trevor made notes while Shea continued the questioning. "You mentioned you're not sad the meetings are on hold. Were other girls feeling the same way?"

"Definitely. Emily Snopes." Kayla's voice caught as she realized what she'd said. "Emily used to complain that it felt more like a cult than a mentoring program. She said Marilyn was obsessed with controlling every aspect of our lives."

"Have you ever noticed anyone hanging around during meetings that made you nervous? Someone who didn't belong?"

Kayla shook her head emphatically. "Marilyn didn't let anyone near the church when there was a meeting. She's very protective, paranoid, even. She'd check all the doors twice and sometimes walk around the building to make sure no one lurked outside."

"Is there something else you want to tell us, Kayla?" Shea had noticed the girl's increasing agitation, the way she kept glancing at the door.

"Well, uh..." Kayla took a deep breath. "This is going to sound crazy, but when we do something against Marilyn's rules, we get these weird text messages. Not from Marilyn herself, but from a number none of us recognize. The texts are always the same theme, telling us that 'the water is always watching' and we need to change our ways or face consequences."

Shea shot Trevor a meaningful look, her pulse quickening. This was the first they'd heard of any direct threats. "Have you personally received one of these texts?"

"Once. After I kissed my boyfriend behind the bleachers during a basketball game, nobody else was around, or so I thought." Kayla's voice dropped to almost a whisper. "The next day, I got a message saying my actions weren't moral and that I needed to stop immediately because 'the water was watching and remembers everything.' It totally creeped me out."

"I can imagine it would. Do you still have the message?"

Kayla pulled up her phone and showed them the text. The message was chilling in its specificity: *Kayla, your behavior tonight was inappropriate and immoral. The water sees all and remembers everything. Change your ways before it's too late.*

"Do you mind if we take a screenshot of that?" Trevor asked, already pulling out his phone.

The remaining girls they interviewed had similar stories about receiving threatening texts, but none had anything new to offer about potential suspects. Each message followed the same pattern: specific knowledge of their private behavior, followed by ominous warnings about "the water watching." Shea wrote down the phone number the texts originated from and handed it to Trevor.

"Find out everything you can about this number.

Registration, location data, anything the phone company will give us," she instructed.

Before they could leave the building, the school receptionist intercepted them in the hallway, her face flushed with worry. "Sheriff, we've got another problem. Two of our students, Olivia Baker and Lauren Mitchell, didn't show up for first period. I called both sets of parents, but they assumed the girls had gotten on the bus as usual. They never made it to school."

Shea felt her stomach drop. "Do you know if either of them was involved in the mentoring program?"

"I checked. Neither girl is on Mrs. Townsend's current list, but Olivia was in the program last year before she quit." The receptionist wrung her hands anxiously. "I know it's still early in the day, but given everything that's been happening, I thought you should know immediately."

"You did exactly the right thing. We need to speak with their friends, anyone who might know where they are."

"I'll send some students to the cafeteria where you can talk privately."

Trevor shoved open the heavy cafeteria doors, his movements sharp with tension. "It's never been two girls at once before. Think they might just be skipping school together?"

"Could be, but we can't take that chance." Shea positioned herself at the front of the large room as four teenage girls filed in, all looking nervous about being called to speak with law enforcement. "Maybe one of their friends will have some insight."

After twenty minutes of questioning, none of the girls could explain why Olivia and Lauren weren't at school. They all insisted it wasn't like either girl to skip classes, especially not without telling their closest friends. Shea decided to inspect their homes personally.

"Let's pay a visit to Lauren's house first. It's closer," she decided.

Lauren Mitchell lived in a modest two-story house on Pine Street, painted yellow with white trim and surrounded by well-tended flower beds. Shea rang the doorbell and waited, noting movement behind the front window curtains. When no one answered after the first ring, she tried again.

"This is Sheriff Callahan. I need someone to open the door."

After a long pause, the door opened just a crack, revealing one frightened brown eye.

"Lauren?"

"Yeah." The girl's voice was barely above a whisper.

"Is Olivia with you? Both your parents and the school are worried sick."

"Yeah, she's here." Lauren's voice trembled. "She's hiding out."

"Let us in, Lauren." Shea kept her voice gentle but firm. "We need to make sure you're both safe."

"Are we in trouble?" The crack in the door

widened slightly.

"That depends on what's going on. But right now, we're more concerned about your safety than any rule-breaking."

Lauren finally opened the door fully, revealing a pale, frightened girl in pajamas who looked like she hadn't slept all night. Inside the living room, another girl sat curled up on the sofa, her knees drawn up to her chest, rocking slightly.

"Trevor, why don't you talk to Lauren in the kitchen?" Shea suggested. "I'll speak with Olivia."

Shea settled on the opposite end of the sofa from Olivia, maintaining a respectful distance. "Mind telling me why you're hiding? You've got quite a few people very concerned about your whereabouts." Not to mention the precious time she needed to spend tracking down a killer.

"I don't want to be the next one to die." Olivia buried her face in her knees, her voice muffled but filled with genuine terror.

"What makes you think you might be in danger?"

"I got a text message." She raised her tear-streaked face, revealing puffy eyes and cheeks flushed from crying. "It was about things I said to my friends. Private things that nobody else should know about."

"Was this during one of the mentoring meetings?"

Olivia shook her head vigorously. "No, I quit the program months ago. It was during lunch at school yesterday. I was telling my friends about sneaking out at night to meet my boyfriend." Her voice broke. "My friends would never snitch on me, Sheriff. They're the only people I told."

"What exactly did the text message say?"

Olivia pulled out her phone, her hands shaking, and showed Shea the screen. The message was more direct and threatening than the others: *Be a good girl, Olivia, or you'll wind up cleansed in the water like Abby and Emily. The water is always watching.*

Shea's blood turned to ice. This wasn't just a vague threat; it was a specific warning that connected the murders directly. "Olivia, listen to me very carefully. You were right to hide today. This message suggests you could very well be the next target."

"But how does the killer know what I said? I only told Lauren and two other friends, and we were alone in the cafeteria." Olivia's voice rose with panic. "Does that mean someone is watching us all the time?"

"We're going to figure that out. But first, we need to get you somewhere safe." Shea stood and extended her hand. "Let's get both of you home to your parents."

"The killer knows where I live," Olivia protested, shrinking back into the sofa cushions.

"We'll make sure you're protected. Come on." Shea's mind raced as she helped the terrified girl to her feet. The killer wasn't acting randomly; they'd already figured that much out. But now it was clear that the perpetrator was selecting victims based on their behavior and somehow had access to their most private conversations. The scope of surveillance was more extensive than they'd imagined.

Back at the station, Shea and Trevor immediately began analyzing the threatening message Olivia had received. Trevor sent the phone number and message content to the county's digital forensics technician with a request for expedited processing.

Three hours later, the technical analysis arrived via secure email. Trevor scanned the detailed report, his expression growing increasingly grim. "It's a prepaid burner phone, just like we suspected. But here's what's interesting. The last signal ping came from Main Street, right in front of the coffee shop. The message was sent the day after Abby was killed."

He spread out a map that the technician had included, where every location where the burner phone had connected to cell towers was circled in red, along with corresponding timestamps. "The signal coverage area includes the entire town of Misty Hollow, so we can't narrow it down to a specific building. But look at the timing pattern."

Shea studied the timestamps carefully. "Every message was sent within hours of a mentoring meeting or right after school let out. Most of them came after evening meetings, though."

"Which suggests the killer has detailed knowledge of the girls' schedules and activities." Trevor leaned back in his chair, running his hands through his hair. "The question is how. Could the killer have a tracking device on their phone? Or maybe recording equipment in places where they gather?"

"With the right technical knowledge, both are possible." Shea felt pieces of the puzzle starting to come together in her mind. "I think we need to search the church. If someone is monitoring these girls' conversations, the mentoring room would be the perfect place to plant surveillance equipment."

Trevor nodded grimly. "I'll start working on getting a search warrant."

Two hours later, they arrived at the church annex with the signed warrant in hand. The main sanctuary was empty except for a few elderly volunteers arranging flowers for Sunday's service. Marilyn was attending a women's ministry event at another church across town, and Pastor Townsend was reportedly at home sick with a severe cold that had kept him bedridden for two days.

Frank Wilson met them at the side entrance, his perpetual scowl even more pronounced than usual. "What's all this about? Can't a man do his work in peace without law enforcement traipsing around?"

"We have a legal warrant to search the premises, Mr. Wilson." Shea showed him the document. "Please unlock any doors we need access to, then make yourself available when we're finished so you can secure the building."

Frank grudgingly led them through the building, unlocking doors and muttering under his breath about harassment and constitutional rights. The church annex contained several small rooms used for Sunday school classes, counseling sessions, and committee meetings.

Trevor headed directly for the room where Marilyn conducted her mentoring sessions. "If there's recording equipment anywhere, it would be in here where the girls feel safe to share personal information."

The room was furnished with a circle of folding chairs, a small table with a wooden cross, and motivational posters about Christian living. But as Shea examined the walls more carefully, something caught her attention.

"Look at this." She pointed to an electrical outlet near the corner where the girls typically sat. "The cover plate isn't sitting flush with the wall. See how it's slightly askew?"

She unhooked a small multi-tool from her key ring and carefully removed the screws holding the outlet cover in place. When the plate came away, a small electronic device fell into her palm, a sophisticated Bluetooth relay with modifications she didn't recognize.

Trevor examined the device closely. "This is high-end surveillance equipment. It can connect to any phone that enters this room, especially if Bluetooth is enabled. But it's been modified with additional components. A micro-storage chip and what looks like a long-range antenna."

"Which means whoever planted this has serious technical skills and regular access to this room." Shea dropped the device into an evidence bag, handling it carefully to preserve any fingerprints.

"That could be a lot of people," Trevor said, looking around the room. "The Townsends obviously have access, Frank Wilson has keys to everything, plus anyone who's been counseled in this room, or really half the church membership."

"Wilson's name keeps coming up in this investigation." Shea sealed the evidence bag and labeled it with the date and location. "But honestly, he doesn't strike me as being particularly tech-savvy. If he is involved, someone with more technical knowledge would have to be helping him."

Trevor's phone buzzed with an incoming call. "It's the forensic analyst again," he said, answering quickly. After a brief conversation, he hung up with new information. "The burner phone briefly connected once to the public Wi-Fi network at the town library. The connection lasted less than five minutes, but it was long enough to send several messages."

"The library is another public place frequented by half the town," Shea sighed. "But it might have security cameras we can check."

As they prepared to leave the church, Trevor spotted something fluttering under the windshield wiper of their patrol car. A church bulletin had been placed there, but someone had written in the margins with black ink: "They all lie. Only the water knows the truth."

Shea stared at the message, feeling a chill run down her spine. "The killer was here. While we were inside searching for evidence, they were outside leaving us another message."

"Which means they're watching our investigation closely," Trevor said grimly. "And they're getting bolder."

Chapter Six

Word spread through Misty Hollow like spilled gasoline catching fire from a tossed cigarette. Frank Wilson had been questioned regarding Abby's death, and the rumors ignited faster than anyone could control them. By eight in the morning, the sheriff's office had received seventeen calls from concerned citizens, each with their theory about the town's groundskeeper.

Some callers claimed they'd seen Frank wandering the woods at all hours of the night, mumbling incoherently about young girls and divine retribution. Others insisted he was nothing more than an eccentric older man who'd been unfairly targeted, and that people should leave him alone before vigilante justice took hold. Mrs. Patterson from the library swore she'd seen him lurking outside the dance studio on multiple occasions. At the same time, her neighbor Carl insisted Frank had helped him fix his lawnmower just last week and seemed perfectly normal.

Shea found herself caught in the middle of one such heated debate during breakfast at Lucy's Diner, trying to eat her eggs in peace while the argument at the next booth grew increasingly animated.

"He's got no alibi for any of the nights those girls disappeared," declared Bob Wilson, a local mechanic, pointing his fork aggressively at his breakfast companion. "That's proof enough for me. Lock him up and throw away the key."

"You ain't got no alibi either, Bob," replied elderly farmer Jim Hendricks, crossing his arms defensively over his flannel shirt. "Hell, none of us do. Maybe they should lock up the whole darn town while they're at it."

Shea nearly choked on her coffee, fighting back an inappropriate laugh. The tension in the community was palpable, but the absurdity of their logic wasn't lost on her.

Bob sputtered indignantly, then tossed his fork onto his plate with a clatter that drew attention from every patron in the small diner. "There's no reasoning with you, Jim. Never has been." He slapped a worn baseball cap on his head and stormed toward the exit, calling over his shoulder, "Lucy, charge this stubborn fool for my breakfast too!"

Despite the humorous nature of the argument, Shea felt the crushing weight of not having a solid suspect press down on her shoulders like a physical burden. As she mechanically worked her way through her breakfast, she noticed several other diners shooting angry glances in her direction. The town loved her most of the time. But when something terrible happened, and she didn't solve it immediately, they turned on her like sharks sensing blood in the water.

The whispered conversations weren't hard to overhear in the small space. "What's taking her so long?" "My daughter's afraid to leave the house." "Maybe we need to bring in the state police." Each comment felt like a small knife between her shoulder blades.

She slapped a ten-dollar bill on the table, grabbed the extra side of bacon she'd ordered for Heidi, and made her escape. In her truck, she handed the dog the treat and then gripped the steering wheel until her knuckles turned white, trying to center herself.

"Today's supposed to be our day off, girl. At least half of it anyway." She looked at Heidi's expectant face in the rearview mirror. "Too much work to stay away from the office all day, but we deserve a few hours to clear our heads. What do you want to do? Go for a walk by the lake?"

The German Shepherd's ears perked up immediately, and her tail wagged against the seat.

"A walk it is, then." Shea started the engine and drove toward Misty Lake, hoping that some fresh air and exercise might help her see something she'd missed in this increasingly complex case. The town counted on her, and she couldn't shake the feeling that another girl's life hung in the balance.

She parked in the main public lot, noting how empty it was compared to normal summer weekends. Word of the murders had clearly impacted tourism, not to mention her shutting the place down. The entire area felt heavy with an oppressive atmosphere that even the bright morning sunshine couldn't dispel.

As they walked along the familiar shoreline trail, Shea tried to organize her thoughts. No one had seen anything suspicious on any of the nights in question. No one had heard screams or calls for help. The girls had essentially vanished and died in a silence so dense that it felt almost supernatural. The killer was either incredibly lucky or extremely skilled at avoiding detection.

Her steps faltered as they neared the spot where Abby's body had been discovered. The crime scene tape was long gone, but she could still visualize exactly how everything had looked that terrible morning. Something caught her attention, a glint of metal partially buried in the muddy shoreline where the gentle waves lapped against the bank.

Pulling on latex gloves she always carried, Shea carefully lifted what appeared to be a bracelet from the mud. She brushed away the dirt and read the engraving on the small nameplate: "Lily Grossman - With Love, Grandma Rose."

Shea frowned as recognition hit her. Lily Grossman wasn't one of the confirmed drowning victims. The fifteen-year-old had disappeared two years ago, but since no body had ever been found, she'd been officially classified as a runaway despite her parents' insistence that she would never have left voluntarily.

How had this piece of jewelry gone unnoticed for so long? Had it been buried in the thick mud at the bottom of the lake, only to be gradually washed free by seasonal water level changes and recent heavy rains? Or had someone deliberately placed it here recently, knowing it would eventually be discovered?

She dropped the bracelet into an evidence bag from her jacket pocket. "Change of plans, Heidi. Time to head to the office. I need to document this evidence properly, then pay an overdue visit to the Grossman family."

Trevor glanced up from his desk when she arrived at the station, squinting at his computer screen with obvious frustration. "Thought you were taking the morning off."

"Was planning to, but I found something important." She held up the evidence bag containing the bracelet. "This belonged to Lily Grossman, the girl who went missing two years ago. Found it at the exact spot where we discovered Abby's body."

Trevor immediately gave her his full attention. "That changes things. Want me to come along when you talk to her parents?"

"Absolutely. I could use the backup, and you're better with grieving families than I am." She moved toward her desk to complete the evidence documentation. "Plus, I'm about to go cross-eyed myself trying to find a solid connection between all these victims. Maybe the Grossmans can provide some insight we've been missing."

The Grossman family lived in a modest country-style house about ten miles outside town, surrounded by sprawling corn fields that stretched to the horizon. A collection of wind chimes hung from the wraparound front porch, creating a gentle, melancholy melody as the afternoon breeze stirred them.

At Trevor's knock, a woman with deep worry lines permanently etched into her forehead answered the door. Despite being only in her early forties, she looked a decade older, aged by the stress of not knowing what had happened to her daughter. Behind her, a television flickered with the sound turned low, and a heavyset man in work clothes sat in a worn recliner, barely acknowledging their presence.

"Sheriff Callahan?" The woman's face immediately paled with renewed fear. "Has something happened? Have you found something about Lily?"

"Mrs. Grossman, I was hoping we could speak with you and your husband for a few minutes. We may have found something that belonged to your daughter."

The woman nodded quickly and stepped aside to let them enter. The living room was tidy but showed signs of a family still frozen in time. Lily's high school graduation photo was prominently displayed on the mantel, despite her disappearance before senior year. At the same time, a partially completed jigsaw puzzle sat on the coffee table, untouched for months.

Mr. Grossman finally looked up from his television program and heaved himself to his feet with apparent reluctance. "Bruce Grossman," he said, crossing his arms defensively. "What's this about? We already told you people everything we know two years ago."

Shea carefully pulled the bagged bracelet from her jacket pocket. "Do either of you recognize this jewelry?"

Mrs. Grossman gasped audibly, her hand flying to her mouth. "Oh my God, that's Lily's bracelet! Her grandmother gave it to her for her thirteenth birthday. It was her most precious possession. She never took it off, not even to shower or sleep." Tears immediately sprang to her eyes. "Where on earth did you find it?"

"At the water's edge of Misty Lake, very close to where we recently found Abby Pearson's body."

Bruce swore under his breath, his face darkening with a mixture of anger and renewed grief. "Still doesn't prove anything definitive. She could've thrown the bracelet away before running off to wherever she went. Kids do crazy things when they're upset."

His wife whirled to face him with more fire than Shea had expected from the seemingly fragile woman. "You know good and well she didn't run away, Bruce Grossman! Lily wasn't that kind of girl. She was responsible, she loved us, and she was excited about her future. She would never have just disappeared without a word."

"Based on everything we've learned about this case," Shea said carefully, "I'm inclined to agree with your wife. I don't believe Lily ran away voluntarily."

"We'd hoped against hope," Mrs. Grossman continued, her hands visibly trembling. "For two whole years, we kept thinking maybe she was out there somewhere, waiting to be found. Maybe she'd lost her memory, or someone was keeping her against her will, but that someday she'd come home." Her voice broke completely. "But finding her bracelet there..."

"You think our daughter was killed by the same monster who murdered the Pearson girl and those others," Mr. Grossman said, his voice flat with resignation. "But without a body, how can you possibly know for certain?"

"We'll be bringing cadaver dogs to search the lake thoroughly," Shea replied gently. "I'm sorry to be the bearer of such difficult news."

"It's not official until my baby is found and brought home," Mrs. Grossman whispered, turning to bury her face against her husband's broad chest as sobs wracked her body.

"I need to ask a few more questions, if you're able to answer them." Shea pulled out her small notepad, hating herself for having to pursue this line of inquiry while the family was in such fresh pain. "In the weeks before Lily disappeared, did she ever mention anyone following her or watching her? Did she seem afraid of anyone specific? And did she have any connection to the local church, the dance studio, or any youth programs run by Marilyn Townsend?"

Mrs. Grossman wiped her eyes and tried to compose herself. "She never mentioned being followed or feeling afraid. Lily was a confident girl, very social. As for church activities..." She paused, thinking carefully. "She did attend some youth group meeting at the church for maybe a week or two before she disappeared. But she quit almost immediately."

"Did she say why she quit?"

"She said the woman running the group made her uncomfortable. Said she wasn't friendly and asked too many personal questions about things that weren't her business. Lily said it felt more like an interrogation than a support group."

Shea exchanged a meaningful look with Trevor as they thanked the Grossmans and made their way back to their patrol car. Once they were out of earshot, Shea voiced what they were both thinking.

"We're spinning our wheels, Trevor. The bodies keep piling up, and we're no closer to stopping this killer than we were when we found Abby." She slammed her car door harder than necessary, frustration boiling over.

"Maybe not, but Marilyn Townsend's name keeps surfacing in every single case. That can't be a coincidence." Trevor started the engine and pulled away from the Grossman house. "We need to keep digging until something breaks open."

"Here's what's bothering me most," Shea said, staring out at the passing cornfields. "This can't just be about the peer mentorship program anymore. Too many of the victims either weren't involved or quit almost immediately. There has to be another connection we're missing. Something that ties all these girls together beyond Marilyn's programs."

"Where do you want to start looking?"

"Back to the high school. I want to speak with the guidance counselor again, go through more records. Maybe there's a pattern in their academic files, or extracurricular activities, or something else entirely."

The school guidance counselor, Mrs. Chance, was happy to help despite the late hour. She directed them to a storage room filled with filing cabinets containing older student records that hadn't yet been digitized.

"I hope you find whatever you're looking for," she said, unlocking the room. "We're slowly trying to get everything transferred to computer files, but it's a massive undertaking with limited budget and staff time."

After an hour of methodical searching through dusty folders and faded documents, Trevor suddenly held up a thick manila folder with obvious excitement. "Bingo. Look at this. Attendance logs for a grief counseling circle that operated here two years ago."

"Let me guess who facilitated it," Shea said,

rushing to peer over his shoulder.

"Marilyn Townsend. And every single one of our victims is listed as a participant." Trevor's voice carried a note of triumph mixed with grim satisfaction. "We finally found the real connection."

Hope leaped in Shea's chest like a flame catching dry kindling. This was the break they'd been desperately searching for.

"Look at this note at the bottom," Trevor continued. "The grief circle was organized completely off-site, not through any official school program. It met at various locations around town; the church, the community center, even private homes."

"Smart move on Marilyn's part. She wouldn't want the restrictions and oversight that came with a school-sponsored program." Shea quickly photographed each page in the folder with her phone. "This way, she had complete control over the participants and the content. No administrators looking over her shoulder, no parents being notified about what was discussed."

Despite the approaching dinner hour, Shea and Trevor drove directly to the church. They found Marilyn in the fellowship hall, methodically arranging folding chairs in a large circle for the evening's women's Bible study. She wore a simple black dress and had pulled her gray hair back in a severe bun that made her already sharp features look even more austere.

Shea didn't waste time with pleasantries. "Mrs.

Townsend, we need to have a serious conversation."

Marilyn straightened slowly, genuine surprise flickering across her face before being quickly masked by her usual composed expression. "I have women arriving in less than an hour for our weekly study. We'll have to make this brief."

She led them to the same small counseling room where they'd discovered the hidden surveillance device. Shea was careful not to glance toward the electrical outlet where they'd found the Bluetooth relay, wondering if anyone had yet noticed the device was missing and what that might mean for their investigation.

Settling into one of the folding chairs, Shea got straight to the point. "You ran a grief counseling group for teenage girls about two years ago."

Marilyn sat across from them and clasped her hands tightly in her lap, her knuckles already showing white from the pressure. "Yes, it was just a small, informal gathering. Similar to an AA meeting, but for troubled girls who needed to talk with others going through similar emotional issues. That's what the church is for, Sheriff...to help those in our community who are struggling and need support."

"Seven girls from that group are now dead. Possibly eight if we include Lily Grossman."

The woman visibly flinched as if she'd been physically slapped. "That many? I... I hadn't realized the number was so high."

"I think you know exactly how many victims there have been." Shea held up a photograph of Lily Grossman from her high school yearbook. "Interesting how this particular girl's name never came up in any of our previous conversations."

"Lily didn't stay with the group long enough to become involved," Marilyn replied, her voice dropping to almost a whisper. "Poor thing felt bullied at school, ignored at home by parents who were too busy with their problems to pay attention to her needs. She should have stayed with us longer. I truly believe I could have helped her work through her issues."

"Lily's bracelet was found in the same spot where we discovered Abby Pearson's body." Trevor's voice was hard with accusation. "Someone has been specifically targeting these girls, Mrs. Townsend. Any idea who that might be?"

Marilyn shook her head, but her hands were now clenched so tightly that her knuckles had turned entirely white. "I don't choose victims, Deputy. These girls came to me seeking help. All I ever did was spread the word that support was available for those who needed it."

"How many of these support groups have you organized over the years?" Trevor asked, crossing his arms and fixing her with a stern stare.

Her mouth opened and closed several times, like a fish gasping for air, but no words came out.

"Enough groups to provide a steady supply of

potential victims?" Trevor raised one eyebrow.

"Don't be ridiculous," Marilyn finally managed to say, though her voice lacked conviction. "I would never deliberately hurt any of those girls. All I've ever wanted was to help them become better people, to find their way back to moral living and spiritual peace."

"Then you must have some idea who might want to harm them," Trevor continued relentlessly. "Someone with access to your meetings, someone who knew these girls' personal struggles and vulnerabilities."

Marilyn's shoulders suddenly slumped as if all the fight had gone out of her. "My brother," she whispered, so quietly they had to strain to hear her. "Elliot visits a few times throughout the year, usually staying with us for several weeks at a time. He... he often watched the meetings from the back of the room, sometimes even interjected with his own perspectives."

A chill ran down Shea's spine as she processed this new information. "You never mentioned having a brother in any of our previous conversations."

"I didn't think it was relevant until this moment. But now that I really think about it..." She trailed off, looking genuinely distressed.

"His full name, Mrs. Townsend."

"Elliot Sweeney. He lives in Langley now, has his own apartment there. He hasn't had to stay with us in over a year because his financial situation improved." Her voice dropped even lower. "But Sheriff, he was always here around the time one of the girls disappeared. I just never made the connection before."

"Why didn't you think to mention this connection earlier?" Shea asked, though she thought she already knew the answer.

"Because he's family. Because he told me he was trying to help these girls, that his own grief over our parents' deaths gave him insight into their pain." Marilyn looked up with tears in her eyes. "I thought his presence was beneficial. I thought wrong."

"Do you have a photograph of your brother?"

"Yes, actually. And I think you'll find it very interesting." She reached into her purse and withdrew a color photograph that had obviously been taken during one of the grief counseling sessions.

The photographer had captured a candid moment during what appeared to be a group discussion. Marilyn stood next to her husband at the front of the room while the teenage girls formed a casual half-circle of chairs around them. But off to one side, partially in shadow, stood another man who looked to be in his forties.

What made Shea's blood run cold was that this man wasn't looking at the camera or participating in the group discussion. Instead, his gaze was fixed intently on the girls with an expression that could only be described as predatory. He had the look of a hunter studying potential prey.

Back in their patrol car, Trevor immediately pulled up official records on Elliot Sweeney while Shea studied the photograph more closely under the car's dome light.

"Here we go," Trevor said grimly. "The guy has a record. He was arrested three years ago for inappropriate behavior toward a minor during a church retreat in another county. A teenage girl complained that he was asking invasive personal questions and trying to get her alone."

"What happened with the charges?"

"They were dropped when the girl's family decided not to pursue prosecution. Sweeney agreed to undergo counseling, but that ended two years ago. Since then, he's been essentially invisible. The man has no social media presence, no credit card usage, no permanent address until recently."

"Yet he came out of hiding specifically to attend his sister's meetings with vulnerable teenage girls." Ssome pieces of the puzzle finally clicked into place.

"And now we have another serious suspect," Trevor concluded, starting the engine.

Another suspect, Shea thought grimly, but still no concrete evidence that would hold up in court. They were getting closer to the truth, but not fast enough to prevent another tragedy if the killer decided to strike again.

Chapter Seven

Shea's radio crackled to life at 5:47 AM, jolting her from a restless sleep filled with nightmares about hooded figures and silent waters. The dispatcher's voice carried an urgency that made her stomach clench with familiar dread.

"Sheriff, we've got another missing girl report. Susie Starling, age sixteen. Parents say she never came home last night and isn't answering her phone."

Shea was already reaching for her uniform, her mind automatically cataloging the patterns: another teenage girl, another sleepless night for another family. "I'll be there in twenty minutes. Have Deputy Bolton meet me at the lake."

Now, an hour later, she stood with Trevor and Heidi once again at the shoreline of Misty Lake, searching for what they all feared would be another body. The morning mist clung to the water's surface like ghostly fingers, and the familiar weight of dread settled on her shoulders. She found herself silently praying that Susie had spent the night with a friend and forgotten to tell her parents—a typical teenage mistake rather than another tragedy.

"Sheriff." A man's voice called out, echoing across the water as someone ran down the main trail toward them.

Trevor's hand instinctively moved to his weapon as he stepped forward and slightly in front of Shea, his protective instincts overriding protocol.

"I've told you repeatedly not to do that." Shea bumped his shoulder with more force than necessary. She hated when he treated her like she needed protection instead of recognizing her as an equal partner capable of handling herself. "We've been through this before."

"Sorry. Old habits die hard," Trevor muttered, though he didn't look particularly apologetic.

"Well, break that particular habit. It's not helpful." She kept her attention focused on the approaching man, noting his agitated body language and rapid pace. "Stop right there, sir, and state your name clearly."

"Dick Kingsley," the man called out, holding his hands visible at his sides in a gesture of non-aggression. He was middle-aged, wearing fishing gear and waterproof boots that suggested he'd been out on the water. "I heard on my ham radio that another girl went missing. Figured you folks would be out here looking for her."

"Why exactly are you out here, Mr. Kingsley?" Shea narrowed her eyes, studying his nervous demeanor and the way his gaze kept darting between her and Trevor.

"Fishing," he replied, though his voice carried a defensive tone. "I know these waters better than most folks, and I thought maybe I could help with the search."

"The entire lake area has been closed to public access for an indefinite period," Shea said firmly. "That includes all recreational activities."

"I thought that restriction only applied to the cabins and campgrounds," he said with a shrug, not appearing the least bit ashamed about fishing in violation of official orders. "Anyway, I thought you might want to know I've been hearing some strange things out here that don't sound natural to these woods. I've also seen footprints around the old camp area—fresh ones that weren't there yesterday."

For someone who claimed to think the restrictions were limited, he'd clearly been exploring the area extensively. "What sort of strange things?" Shea asked, growing tired of his evasive answers.

"I've been hearing crying coming from the direction of the old cabins. Sounds like a young woman in distress. But when I go to investigate and see if someone needs help, I never find anyone there. The crying just stops." He paused, glancing nervously toward the wooded area. "And I'm not talking about the newer rental cabins that are still in use. This is coming from the ones that haven't been occupied in years."

"Mr. Kingsley, I'm going to tell you one more time that this entire area is off-limits to civilians. Thank you for reporting what you've observed, but Deputy Bolton and I will handle the investigation from here. Please leave the area immediately and don't return until we've officially reopened it."

"Excuse me for trying to be a good citizen and help out," he said with obvious irritation, scowling as he turned and marched toward a small aluminum boat equipped with a trolling motor.

Shea watched carefully until the man had nearly reached the opposite shore, making sure he was actually leaving the area. "Let's check out those old cabins he mentioned. If someone is using them as a hideout, we need to know about it."

The abandoned cabins were located behind a section of rusted barbed wire fencing that had clearly seen better days. Multiple signs hung from the deteriorating fence. An official No Trespassing notice from the county and a faded wooden sign that read "Camp Misty" in cheerful letters that seemed almost mocking in the current circumstances.

"I remember this place," Trevor said, studying the crumbling structures. "It was an old church camp that operated here for decades. I actually attended summer camp here when I was about ten, before my family moved away from Misty Hollow. I heard it closed down about ten years ago due to a lack of funding and insurance liability issues. No idea why the county hasn't ordered the buildings demolished. They're a safety hazard."

The first few cabins they checked showed obvious signs of recent habitation by transients and drug users. Cabin number three contained the remnants of a small campfire in the center of what had once been the main living area, with the ashes appearing no more than a day old. Empty beer bottles, discarded food containers, and drug paraphernalia littered the warped wooden floors.

"Looks like the homeless population and local addicts have discovered these buildings," Shea observed grimly. "I'll need to speak with the city council about getting these structures torn down before someone gets seriously hurt or we have more problems."

Cabin number six proved more interesting. Near the back wall, they discovered a cracked cell phone with a distinctive pink case. While the screen was spider-webbed with damage, it wasn't broken enough to hide the lock screen wallpaper of a photo of a teenage girl with long brown hair and a bright smile.

"That's Susie Starling," Trevor confirmed, comparing the image to the missing person photo they'd been given. "But look at this…there's a fast-food bag in the corner, and two empty paper cups on the windowsill. The food containers are from yesterday, based on the receipt."

"I seriously doubt our killer would sit down to enjoy a meal with a victim he was planning to murder." Shea examined the scene more carefully. "Which means Susie wasn't alone when she came here. She was with someone. Probably a boyfriend, given the two drinks."

She stepped out the back door of the cabin, scanning the surrounding forest for any sign of where Susie might have gone. "The question is, where are you now, Susie?"

"Shea, you need to see this immediately," Trevor called from inside the cabin.

She followed his voice back into the structure and through a doorway that led to a tiny bathroom with a cracked mirror and broken fixtures. Written across the mirror's surface in black marker was a single word that made her blood run cold: "Obedience."

Her heart sank as the implications hit her. Susie might have come to this isolated cabin with a friend for innocent reasons, but it was increasingly likely that the killer had followed them here or discovered them after they arrived.

"Is there another significant body of water nearby besides the creek that runs into the lake?" she asked, trying to think like the killer.

"Not really," Trevor said, shaking his head. "The creek is the closest water source to this location. If Susie was taken from here, that's probably where we should focus our search efforts."

"Lead the way, then."

They left the cabin area and headed into the dense forest that surrounded the abandoned church camp. The silence that hung over the thick woods felt oppressive and unnatural. Ancient moss carpeted the forest floor, muffling their footsteps and creating an eerie, cathedral-like atmosphere beneath the towering pines.

Trevor suddenly stopped so abruptly that Shea nearly collided with him. "Shh." He pointed ahead through the trees. "Movement up there."

About fifty yards ahead, the shadows seemed to shift and coalesce into a darker shape that didn't belong to the natural forest environment. As they watched, the shadow moved deliberately to the left and disappeared behind a cluster of massive oak trees.

Someone watched them, and that someone clearly didn't want to be seen.

Shea reached for her service weapon and drew it from its holster, keeping the barrel pointed down but ready. "We need to split up," she whispered into Trevor's ear. "We can't let this person escape. They might be our only link to finding Susie alive. Keep your radio on and maintain contact."

Trevor nodded grimly and veered left toward where they'd last seen the mysterious figure. Shea took the right flank, hoping to circle and cut off any escape route through the denser part of the forest.

Moving off the main trail onto what appeared to be

an old deer path, Shea found the going much more treacherous. Exposed tree roots threatened to trip her with every step, and the thick canopy overhead blocked out most of the morning sunlight, creating an almost twilight atmosphere that made it difficult to see clearly. The narrow path curved and twisted through the undergrowth, gradually leading her in what she hoped was the right direction toward the creek.

When she finally stepped into a small clearing about ten minutes later, she immediately sensed something was wrong. Trevor's heavy-duty flashlight lay abandoned near the base of a large pine tree, and the metal casing was smeared with what was unmistakably blood.

Her heart rate spiked as she followed a clear set of drag marks through the carpet of pine needles and fallen leaves. "Trevor!" she called into her radio, but received nothing except static in response.

A sharp whistling sound cut through the forest silence, followed immediately by a metallic snap that seemed to explode from directly beneath her feet.

Before she could react, a steel cable snare yanked her left leg upward with tremendous force, tightening around her ankle and hoisting her into the air like a piece of game. Her breath rushed from her lungs as momentum slammed her sideways into the rough bark of a tree trunk. The impact sent her radio tumbling to the forest floor, where it landed with a crack that suggested it was now useless.

She hung there upside down, the world spinning around her as blood rushed to her head and panic began clawing up her spine. The steel cable bit into her ankle through her boot, and she could feel it cutting off circulation. This was exactly the kind of trap a hunter would set for large game…or for a human being.

No. Get it together, she told herself firmly. She'd been in challenging situations before and survived through clear thinking and determination. Panic would only make things worse.

Using her core strength and the flexibility training she'd maintained since her military days, she slowly pulled herself upward until she could reach the tactical knife strapped to her leg. Just as her fingers closed around the handle, the sound of deliberate footsteps crunching through the underbrush made her freeze.

The footsteps were slow and measured, clearly belonging to someone who was taking their time and enjoying the situation. Someone who wanted her to know they were coming.

A hooded figure wearing a black ski mask stepped into the clearing, moving with the confidence of someone who had planned this encounter carefully. In one gloved hand, the person carried a stun gun that gleamed in the filtered sunlight. When their eyes met through the mask's openings, Shea realized with sudden clarity that this was not a man staring up at her.

The figure was female despite the baggy clothing worn in an apparent attempt to disguise her actual shape and size. The body language, the way she held herself, even the deliberate manner of her approach—everything screamed "woman" to Shea's trained eye.

The killer slowly raised the stun gun, clearly intending to incapacitate her before doing whatever came next.

A gunshot suddenly rang out through the forest, the sound echoing off the trees and causing birds to explode from their roosts in a flurry of wings and alarm calls.

The hooded woman whirled toward the sound and immediately melted back into the shadows between the trees like smoke, disappearing with a speed that suggested extensive familiarity with these woods.

A few heartbeats later, Trevor stumbled into view from behind a massive oak tree. One hand was pressed against his bleeding forehead, while the other gripped his service pistol. His uniform was torn and dirty, and he moved like someone fighting off a concussion.

"Shea!" he gasped, rushing forward despite his obvious injuries.

Shea quickly sliced through the steel cable with her knife and dropped to the ground, her shoulder taking the brunt of the impact. Pain shot through her joint, but she forced herself to focus on the important information. "Trevor, listen to me. Our killer is a woman. I'm absolutely certain of it. The body language, the size, everything about the person who just tried to stun me screams female."

Trevor's face paled as he processed this revelation. "She got the jump on me about fifteen minutes ago. Hit me from behind with something heavy. Probably a branch or a rock. I went down hard and smacked my head against that tree trunk. Next thing I knew, I was waking up in a pile of dead leaves with my head pounding like a bass drum."

"This changes everything about our investigation." Shea retrieved her pistol from where it had fallen and checked to make sure it hadn't been damaged. "We need to start looking at this case with completely fresh eyes. Marilyn Townsend just moved to the top of our suspect list."

"Either that, or our real killer wants us to think it's Marilyn and has been setting her up from the beginning." Trevor wiped blood from his forehead with his sleeve.

"That's definitely another viable possibility we need to consider."

They spent another hour searching the immediate area but found no additional evidence that Susie had been brought to this location. As they made their way back toward their patrol car, Trevor's radio crackled with an incoming message from dispatch.

"All units, be advised that Susie Starling has returned home safely. Parents report she arrived about twenty minutes ago and appears unharmed."

"Well, that's the best news we've had all day" Trevor snapped his seatbelt into place. "Let's visit Susie and see what she can tell us about her adventure. She might have seen our hooded woman."

"First, we're stopping by the emergency room to have a doctor look at that head injury," Shea said firmly, starting the engine. "You could have a concussion, and I'm not taking any chances."

"I'm fine, really. We can't afford to let time pass when we're this close to a breakthrough. Every minute we delay gives our killer more time to plan her next move."

"There are some antiseptic wipes in the glove compartment. At least clean the blood off your face before we interview Susie." She pulled up the Starling family's address in the car's computer system and headed in that direction, making a mental note to insist on medical attention for Trevor as soon as they finished this interview.

Mrs. Starling answered the front door before they could even knock, clearly having been watching for their arrival. "I suppose you're here to talk to my delinquent daughter about her little disappearing act."

"Yes, ma'am. We also found this at the old church camp." Shea handed the woman Susie's cracked cell phone, watching her face for any reaction.

"She's waiting in the living room, and she knows she's in serious trouble." Mrs. Starling led them into a modest but well-kept room where she positioned herself with arms crossed, glaring at her daughter. "Tell them exactly why you had the entire town out searching for you."

"I spent the night at the lake with my boyfriend," Susie mumbled, not making eye contact with any of the adults in the room.

"Speak up so everyone can hear you," her mother demanded.

Susie cleared her throat and repeated herself, this time loud enough to be understood clearly.

"Was someone else out there with you, Susie?" Shea asked, settling into a chair across from the teenager. "Someone you didn't invite or expect to see?"

The girl's head whipped around to face her, eyes wide with surprise. "How did you know that? Did someone see us?"

"Call it professional intuition. Did you get a good look at this person? Would you be able to recognize them if you saw them again?" Shea held up a hand to prevent Susie's mother from interrupting with more scolding.

The teenager took a deep, shuddering breath and then continued. "This morning, I got up early to use the bathroom in one of the old cabins. At first, I didn't think anything about the word someone had written on the mirror. I was still half asleep and figured it was just old graffiti. But I asked Jacob if he'd written it, and he said he hadn't."

"What did you do then?"

"I stepped outside onto the front porch to get some fresh air and wake up properly. That's when I saw... it."

Her voice dropped to almost a whisper.

"Take your time and tell us exactly what you saw."

"Someone dressed completely in black, standing at the edge of the tree line just watching our cabin. They had on a hood that covered their face, so I couldn't tell if it was a man or woman, but something about the way they stood there felt really threatening." Susie's hands began to shake as she relived the memory. "Jacob came out onto the porch behind me, took one look at the figure, and immediately pulled me back inside the cabin."

"What happened next?"

"Jacob told me we needed to leave immediately through the back door. I dropped my phone in my hurry to grab our stuff, and then I accidentally stepped on it, which is why it's all cracked up. We ran out the back and into the woods as fast as we could. I heard footsteps behind us. Whoever it was followed us into the forest."

Tears trailed down Susie's cheeks as the full impact of her close call hit her. "That was the same person who killed Abby and those other girls, wasn't it? I could have died this morning if Jacob hadn't been there to help me escape."

"My poor baby," Mrs. Starling said, her anger immediately replaced by maternal concern as she gathered her daughter into a protective embrace. "This is exactly why I need to always know where you are and who you're with."

A young man who appeared to be about eighteen

entered the room, clearly having been waiting nearby.

"You must be Jacob," Shea said, sizing up the boyfriend who had potentially saved Susie's life.

"Yes, ma'am," he replied respectfully. "Jacob Martinez. Everything Susie told you is exactly what happened. That person in black was stalking us, and they followed us when we ran into the woods."

"The two of you were extremely lucky to escape," Shea said seriously. "Susie, I need to ask you something important. Do you belong to any groups or clubs run by Marilyn Townsend? Have you ever participated in any of her counseling sessions?"

Susie's eyes widened with obvious recognition. "I'd asked about joining the Peer Mentor Program, but Mrs. Townsend said it was shut down temporarily. She told me she'd let me know when it started back up and that I'd be a perfect candidate for the group."

"We did see someone else out there," Jacob added. "There was a homeless-looking guy staying in one of the other cabins. I caught him watching us a few times during the night, but he never approached us or tried to get close."

"Have you ever seen this homeless man before?" Trevor asked.

"Once, I think. He hangs around the gas station on Highway 34 sometimes. The night attendant there is really nice and sometimes gives food to people who need it."

Shea nodded, making a mental note to check out

the gas station later. She turned back to Susie with one final question. "Did you know Abby Pearson very well? Were you close friends?"

"We were friends, but not best friends or anything like that. We hung out occasionally and talked at school." Susie paused, seeming to consider whether to share something else. "If you want to know her real secrets, you should ask her mother about Abby's journal. She kept a detailed diary and wrote in it almost every day. Maybe her mom has found it by now."

"What kind of secrets do you think might be in her journal?"

"I think Abby was seeing someone romantically. Someone she didn't want her mother to know about. She'd been acting kind of secretive lately, always texting someone and smiling about it."

Shea exchanged a meaningful look with Trevor. This was potential crucial information they hadn't uncovered before.

"Thank you both for being so helpful," she said, rising from her chair. "You've provided some very important information for our investigation."

Outside, she turned to Trevor with renewed energy. "Do you have enough stamina left to visit the Pearson home again and then check out that gas station Jacob mentioned?"

"I'll go as long as it takes to bring down this killer," he replied with a grin that didn't quite mask his obvious fatigue and lingering headache.

Shea nodded with determination. She felt the same way. They would pursue every lead and work around the clock if necessary. When they returned to the office later, she was also going to make the call she'd been avoiding. It was time to contact the FBI and request federal assistance with this case. The killer was becoming bolder and more dangerous, and they needed all the resources they could get to stop her before she claimed another victim.

Chapter Eight

A heavy cloud of grief hung over the Pearson house like a suffocating blanket when Shea and Trevor arrived. The normally well-tended flower beds looked wilted and neglected, and the cheerful yellow paint on the shutters seemed to have dulled in the weeks since Abby's death. Even the wind chimes on the front porch hung motionless in the still air, as if the house itself was holding its breath.

Abby's mother answered the door wearing the same haunted expression Shea had seen on too many bereaved parents over the years. Her hair was uncombed, her clothes wrinkled, and dark circles under her eyes suggested she hadn't been sleeping well. The vibrant woman they'd met weeks ago had been replaced by a hollow shell going through the motions of living.

"I don't think Abby kept a journal," Mrs. Pearson said, her voice barely above a whisper as she dabbed at her eyes with a tissue that had seen heavy use. "But I haven't had the courage to go through her room yet. I just haven't had the heart. It's too soon, and I keep thinking that if I don't disturb anything, maybe she'll somehow come back."

"We understand how difficult this must be, ma'am." Shea's own heart ached for the woman's obvious pain. "Do you mind if we take a look? If there's anything in her room that might help us find out who killed her, even the smallest clue could make a difference."

"Not at all. If there's anything—anything at all—in her room that will help you find the monster who took my baby from me, I'm willing to do almost anything." Mrs. Pearson's voice strengthened slightly with maternal determination. "She's upstairs, first door on the right. The room with the sunflower stickers on the door. I've got to run an errand at the pharmacy—I can't seem to get through the day without something to help me sleep. Just pull the front door closed when you leave."

Shea and Trevor climbed the narrow staircase, each creak of the old wooden steps sounding unnaturally sharp in the oppressive quiet of the house. Family photos lined the stairway wall—Abby at various ages, school pictures, dance recitals, family vacations at the lake that now seemed tragically ironic. The progression of images told the story of a happy, normal childhood cut brutally short.

Abby's bedroom door hung open, and afternoon

sunlight filtered through gauzy white curtains, casting a soft, ethereal glow over the space that made it feel almost shrine-like. The room was a fascinating blend of teenage whimsy and personal sanctuary that spoke volumes about the girl who had lived there. Photos were taped haphazardly to the vanity mirror—friends making silly faces, school events, dance performances. Posters of popular movie stars and musicians covered most of the wall space, creating a collage of teenage dreams and aspirations. A stack of well-worn young adult fantasy novels sat on the nightstand next to a reading lamp and a half-empty water glass. Makeup and jewelry scattered across the vanity surface suggested their owner had stepped out for a moment and would return any minute.

While Trevor moved methodically toward the walk-in closet to begin his search there, Shea's trained gaze swept over every inch of the room. The cluttered desk with homework assignments still waiting to be completed, the unmade bed with its colorful quilt folded neatly at the foot, the bulletin board covered with ticket stubs and mementos. The girl seemed to have been an interesting mixture of organized and chaotic, with some areas meticulously arranged while others showed the typical teenage disregard for order.

A photograph protruding slightly from the pages of one of the novels caught Shea's attention. With a gloved hand, she carefully pulled it free and studied the image. It was a candid shot of Abby with a young man, both of them laughing at something off-camera, their shoulders touching in an intimate way that suggested more than friendship. Unfortunately, the boy had turned his head at just the wrong moment, making it impossible to get a clear look at his facial features.

"This could be important." Shea slipped the photo into an evidence bag. "Abby definitely had a secret relationship with someone."

Frowning with concentration, she continued her methodical search of the room. "Finding anything interesting in there?"

"Not yet," Trevor answered from the depths of the closet. "Although I can tell you that this girl had a serious obsession with the color blue. I'd say ninety percent of her clothes are some shade of blue—navy, powder blue, royal blue, you name it. Her mother wasn't exaggerating when she said it was Abby's favorite color."

"Hmm." Shea was examining the area near the window when something caught her eye. At the edge of the room, beneath a cushioned window seat that overlooked the backyard, she spotted faint scuff marks on the wooden floorboards. The marks looked fresh and seemed oddly out of place in a room where everything else appeared undisturbed.

Kneeling, she ran her fingers along the base of the window seat paneling. One section felt different from the rest—slightly loose, with a barely perceptible gap that wouldn't be noticeable unless someone was looking for it. She applied gentle pressure, and a small section of the panel gave way, revealing a hidden compartment.

"Trevor, I found something significant."

Nestled inside the secret space, wrapped protectively in a soft blue t-shirt, was a small spiral-bound diary with a fabric cover decorated with tiny, embroidered flowers. The edges of the pages were worn from frequent handling, and some of the ink had begun to smudge, suggesting the journal had been well-used and treasured.

"This is exactly what we needed." Shea carefully extracted the diary from its hiding place.

She opened to the first page and began reading. Initially, the entries contained typical teenage concerns—school events, frustrations with parents, friendship drama, worries about upcoming tests. These were the kinds of things that seemed monumentally crucial to a young person but would appear trivial to adult eyes. However, as Shea continued reading chronologically, a noticeable shift in tone began to emerge around three months before Abby's death.

March 15th - There's someone I've been seeing, someone special. Mom and Dad would totally freak out if they knew about him. He's a little older than me, but that doesn't matter at all. Age is just a number anyway. He's so different from the immature boys at school who only want to talk about sports and video games. He's mature, sophisticated, worldly. When I talk, he really listens to what I'm saying instead of just waiting for his turn to speak. He asks thoughtful questions about my dreams and my feelings, not like the boys at school who only talk about themselves and never seem interested in anyone else's thoughts.

Shea continued reading, noting how Abby's handwriting became more animated and excited as she described her secret romance.

March 28th - We've been meeting at the old, abandoned gas station on Highway 64. Nobody hardly goes there anymore since the new station was built closer to town. There's this rickety wooden bench out behind the building where we sit and talk for hours. Sometimes, when we're there together watching the sunset, it feels like we're the only two people left in the entire world. He tells me things about his life, about his past, but I can tell he's holding back some crucial secrets. That just makes him more attractive and exciting to me. I think I'm really falling in love for the first time in my life.

The entries continued in this vein for several weeks, with Abby describing clandestine meetings, stolen kisses, and the intoxicating feeling of being involved in a forbidden romance. But as Shea read further, she began to notice subtle changes in the tone— hints of uncertainty and growing concern creeping into Abby's normally effusive descriptions.

The final entry was dated just two days before Abby's body had been discovered at the lake.

April 10th - Something was different about him

today. He seemed upset, nervous, and almost paranoid about something. He kept looking around like he thought someone might be watching us. He told me that people would never understand our relationship if they found out about us, that there were things about his past that could cause problems. He made me promise to be extra careful about who I trust, but I'm not sure exactly what he meant by that. I promised him I'd keep our relationship completely secret, but I already messed up. I let it slip to someone I thought I could trust. I hope I didn't make a terrible mistake.

"This is crucial information," Trevor said, reading over Shea's shoulder. "I wonder who she told about the relationship. It could be that the person is our killer, or maybe this secret boyfriend killed her to prevent her from revealing his identity. Maybe he shared those secrets he was hiding and then realized she was a liability."

As Shea started to turn toward the bedroom door, a distinct floorboard creak echoed from the hallway outside the room. The sound was deliberate and heavy, definitely caused by human footsteps rather than the natural settling of an old house. Her hand went instinctively to her sidearm as years of training kicked in.

"Mrs. Pearson?" she called out, though something in her gut told her the grieving mother wasn't back from her errand yet.

Trevor immediately understood the situation. He

put a finger to his lips for silence and tiptoed to the bedroom door, withdrawing his service weapon as he moved. Peering cautiously around the doorframe, he suddenly shouted, "Stop! Police! Don't move."

Without hesitation, he darted from the room with Shea close behind. They caught a brief glimpse of a figure dressed entirely in black rushing down the stairs and bolting out the front door. The person moved with surprising speed and agility, clearly familiar with the house's layout and having planned this intrusion carefully.

They pursued the intruder across the front yard and toward the railroad tracks that ran behind the Pearson property. The black-clad figure barely made it across the tracks before a freight train came roaring past, its whistle blaring and effectively cutting off any chance of pursuit. By the time the long train had passed, their quarry had vanished entirely.

Trevor holstered his weapon. "Whoever that was knew we were here and specifically came to stop us from finding that diary."

"Which means our killer knows we have Abby's journal now," Shea said grimly. "This investigation just became significantly more dangerous for everyone involved."

"We couldn't get a clear look at the person. Could have been male or female based on the build and the way they moved," Trevor replied. "But the fact that they were watching this house suggests they're local and have been monitoring our investigation."

"Let's get this diary back to the station for proper evidence processing, then head to that gas station. We need to find this mystery boyfriend and get some answers."

The abandoned gas station on Highway 64 looked like a relic from a bygone era. The old-fashioned pumps stood like rusted sentinels, their price displays frozen at numbers that hadn't been relevant for over a decade. Weeds grew up through cracks in the asphalt, and graffiti covered most of the exterior walls. Despite its run-down appearance, the station was still technically operational, serving the occasional customer who needed gas or basic supplies.

A middle-aged man with graying hair and calloused hands sat behind the counter inside the small convenience store attached to the station. He was flipping through a hunting magazine with apparent boredom, barely glancing up when Shea and Trevor entered and activated the door's electronic chime.

"We're looking for information about a young man who used to meet with a teenage girl on the bench behind your building." Shea displayed her badge.

The man's demeanor immediately became more attentive and cooperative. "Oh, you must be looking for Landon Spencer. That boy's been coming around here for months, always meeting with some young lady or another. He's been really down in the dumps since that Pearson girl was found dead. Keeps saying he should have protected her somehow. Poor kid's been beating himself up something fierce."

"Where might we find Mr. Spencer now?" Trevor asked.

"He lives in an old RV parked out behind the building. Been renting the space from me for about six months now. Pays his rent on time and doesn't cause any trouble, so I don't ask too many questions about his business."

Outside the station, Shea asked Trevor to run a quick background check on Landon Spencer while they walked toward the RV.

"Here's what I've got," Trevor said, scrolling through information on his phone. "Landon Spencer, age nineteen, graduated from Misty Hollow High School two years ago. He's had some minor run-ins with the law—trespassing, underage drinking, public disturbance—but nothing violent in his record. Seems like typical young adult rebellion rather than serious criminal behavior."

"Still, there's always a first time for escalation. Though honestly, I don't think Landon killed Abby. The bigger question is what would be his motive for targeting all the other girls? There doesn't seem to be any connection."

They approached an older model RV that had seen better days. The exterior was faded and showed signs of weather damage, but it appeared to be well-maintained and in good working order. A young man knelt beside a bicycle, working on repairing a broken chain.

"Landon Spencer?" Shea called out. "I'm Sheriff Callahan, and this is Deputy Bolton. We'd like to ask you some questions."

The young man looked up from his repair work. Shea was struck by the genuine sadness that clouded his otherwise handsome features. His dark hair was disheveled, his clothes wrinkled, and his eyes held the kind of grief that couldn't be faked.

"You're here about Abby," he said quietly. "She didn't deserve what happened to her. Abby was the sweetest, most innocent girl I've ever known. Whoever killed her is a monster."

"We'd like to hear about your relationship with her." Shea settled onto the weathered wooden bench where the secret meetings had taken place. "We found her diary, and she wrote extensively about meeting someone here. She mentioned keeping the relationship secret."

"Yeah, we'd been seeing each other for about three months," Landon confirmed, wiping his greasy hands on a dirty rag. "It was my idea to keep things quiet. I know I have a reputation around town as a bit of a troublemaker, and Abby was still underage. I didn't want people getting the wrong idea or causing problems for her with her parents."

He paused, his voice becoming thick with emotion. "But I want you to know that I would never, ever hurt her. I loved that girl more than I've ever loved anyone in my life. She was planning to wait for me, maybe go to college nearby so we could keep seeing each other."

"Where were you on the night Abby disappeared?" Trevor pulled out his notebook.

"I was at my cousin's house on the other side of town, playing video games with him and a couple of his friends. We were up until almost three in the morning. You can check with them. They'll verify my alibi."

"We'll definitely do that," Shea assured him. "Is there anything else you can tell us about Abby's state of mind in the days before she died? Did she seem worried or frightened about anything?"

Landon's expression grew troubled. "Actually, yes. The last time I saw her—which was about three days before she died—Abby told me she felt like someone had been following her around town. She said she'd noticed the same dark SUV behind her on several different occasions, and it was making her nervous."

"Did she get a good look at the driver?"

"No, the windows were tinted too dark. She thought maybe it was her parents having her followed because they suspected she was seeing someone. Lots of parents do that when they get suspicious about their kids' behavior." He wiped away tears that had started flowing down his cheeks. "I told her it was probably just paranoia, that lots of people in town drive dark SUVs. Maybe I should have taken her concerns more seriously. If I had insisted she tell her parents or go to the police, maybe she'd still be alive."

"You can't blame yourself for what happened," Shea said gently. "Evil people make their own choices, and there's no way you could have predicted this."

As they prepared to leave, Landon called out to them. "I should probably mention that there's a homeless guy named Ben who comes by here about once a week. He's been drifting through town for years, mostly harmless, but he always seems very interested in the young people who hang around here. Might be worth talking to him."

"Thank you for the information," Shea replied. "If you think of anything else, please call us immediately."

Back at the sheriff's office, Trevor quickly verified Landon's alibi, which checked out completely. His cousin and two friends all confirmed that Landon had been with them playing video games until the early morning hours on the night Abby disappeared.

"So, what's our next move?" Shea asked, rubbing her temples where a stress headache was beginning to build.

"How about dinner?" Trevor suggested with a grin. "I know, I know—you're going to ask if there's ever a minute when I'm not thinking about food."

"Actually, you read my mind," she said with a slight smile. "But you're right that we both need to eat, and maybe we can gather some information about this drifter Ben while we're at Lucy's Diner. There's not much that happens in this town that the regular customers there don't know about."

"Sounds like a plan. I'll meet you there so we can head to our respective homes afterward."

"Come on, Heidi," Shea called to her German Shepherd. "We've been apart too long today, and I don't want to leave you alone anymore. This case is getting too dangerous to take any chances."

At Lucy's Diner, Shea parked close enough to the large front windows that Heidi could see her clearly from inside the restaurant. She chose a booth with a clear view of the entrance so she could observe anyone who entered the establishment. The diner was moderately busy for a weeknight, with the usual mix of local families, truckers passing through, and elderly regulars who treated the place like their personal social club.

Since she wasn't as familiar with the local characters as Trevor was, Shea ordered the chicken fried steak dinner and settled back to watch as he approached a couple of older men sitting at the counter. These were the kind of longtime residents who seemed to know everyone's business and were usually happy to share information with law enforcement.

As she waited for her meal, Shea reflected on how hard she and Trevor had been working every single day since Abby's body was discovered, yet they seemed no closer to identifying the killer than they'd been on day one. As a former homicide detective with the state police, she'd built her reputation on solving difficult cases and bringing killers to justice. She had no intention of letting this be the first case that defeated her.

Her attention was drawn to the front entrance as Pastor Townsend and his wife Marilyn entered the diner. Marilyn's eyes immediately found Shea's, and she shot her a quick, calculating glance before her gaze shifted to Trevor at the counter. Then she followed her husband to a table on the far side of the restaurant, but Shea noticed how she positioned herself to keep both law enforcement officers in her line of sight.

As Shea got deeper into this investigation, her suspicions about Marilyn Townsend continued to grow stronger. Either the woman knew significantly more than she was admitting, or she was directly responsible for killing those girls. The psychology made sense in a twisted way. Marilyn had lost her only child to drowning, so she understood intimately how devastating that loss felt for parents. Perhaps something had snapped in her mind, triggering her to kill again and again in some warped attempt to recreate or process her own daughter's death.

Marilyn had positioned herself as a mentor and counselor to vulnerable young girls, gaining their trust and learning their secrets. The killer specifically targeted girls who broke "the rules". Girls who engaged in behavior that Marilyn would consider immoral or inappropriate. And Marilyn's own daughter Bella had died after sneaking out against her parents' wishes, which seemed like too much of a coincidence.

Trevor slid into the booth across from her, interrupting her dark thoughts. "Good news about the drifter. Those gentlemen at the counter confirmed that Ben has been passing through Misty Hollow regularly for several years. They all agree that he's essentially harmless, just a wanderer who doesn't cause trouble."

"Still doesn't hurt to track him down and interview him. At this point, we can't afford to leave any lead unexplored, no matter how unlikely it seems."

After finishing their meals, Shea climbed into her truck, tossed two hamburgers to Heidi as a late dinner, and began the drive home. Her mind continued clicking through all the unanswered questions and missing pieces of information that were preventing them from solving this case.

She was about halfway home when bright headlights suddenly appeared in her rearview mirror, approaching fast and getting uncomfortably close to her rear bumper. The lights were positioned high off the ground, suggesting a large SUV or pickup truck, and they appeared to have their high beams on, creating a blinding glare that made it difficult for her to see the road ahead clearly.

Shea flashed her own lights in the universal signal for the other driver to back off and dim their headlights. When the driver not only ignored her warning but actually moved even closer, she realized this wasn't an accident or a case of inconsiderate driving. Someone was deliberately trying to intimidate or provoke her.

"If you want to play games, I'm more than happy to play." She increased her speed and prepared for evasive maneuvers.

She took the next corner faster than was strictly safe, then whipped her steering wheel hard to the left, positioning her truck sideways across both lanes of the narrow country road, effectively blocking any passage. By the time the pursuing vehicle came around the corner, Shea was standing beside her truck with her service weapon drawn and aimed directly at the approaching headlights.

"Get out of the vehicle with your hands visible!"

Instead of complying, the other vehicle's engine revved loudly, and it began backing up rapidly. The driver attempted to execute a quick three-point turn to escape, but their driving skills were nowhere near as advanced as Shea's. The vehicle ended up sliding sideways into the roadside ditch, where it became stuck in the soft mud.

"Come, girl!" Shea called to Heidi. "Get ready to pursue."

A figure wearing dark jeans and a black hoodie burst from the disabled vehicle and sprinted toward the tree line. Shea gave chase, her police training and adrenaline allowing her to maintain a surprising pace despite the uneven terrain.

"Stop! Police!" She fired a warning shot into the air.

The fleeing figure ignored her commands and

continued running through the dense forest. When they reached the bank of Misty Lake, the person dove into a small motorboat that had been positioned there in advance as an escape route. The boat's engine roared to life, and within seconds, the mysterious driver sped across the dark water toward the opposite shore.

Heidi barked frantically at the water's edge, clearly frustrated by her inability to continue the pursuit.

"Easy, girl. We lost them this time." Shea sighed as she holstered her weapon.

Another close encounter that had resulted in absolutely nothing concrete. Whoever was behind these incidents was definitely in better physical condition than she was, and they clearly knew the local area well enough to plan elaborate escape routes.

Standing there in the darkness beside the lake where so many young lives had been lost, Shea made a firm resolution. It was time to get back into the physical condition that had served her so well during her days as a state police officer. Tomorrow morning, she would resume the regular jogging routine she'd maintained for years before this case had disrupted every aspect of her life.

This investigation was far from over, and she had a feeling the killer was just getting started with their psychological games.

Chapter Nine

Trevor shot Shea several pointed side glances the next morning as they drove toward The Fill 'Er Up gas station on Highway 34. His jaw clenched with obvious frustration, and he'd been unusually quiet during their morning briefing at the station.

"Why didn't you call me last night? Why wait until this morning to tell me you had a dangerous confrontation with a potential killer?" His voice carried the edge of someone who felt betrayed by his partner's failure to communicate. "You could have been seriously hurt, or worse."

"I handled the situation ." Shea's irritation started to surface. He really needed to stop trying to act like her protective guardian. She glanced back at Heidi, who was alert in the rear seat. "I already have one protector, thank you very much."

"There's a serial killer operating in Misty Hollow, Shea. Someone who's already murdered at least six young women, probably more, and is clearly escalating their behavior. This isn't the time for unnecessary risks or lone-wolf heroics."

"I'm fully aware of the situation, Trevor. I'm hunting this killer right alongside you every single day." She pulled into the gas station parking lot and cut the engine with more force than necessary. "I appreciate your concern—I genuinely do—but I can take care of myself. I've been doing it successfully for years. I told you about last night's encounter this morning because you needed to know. End of discussion."

Trevor looked like he wanted to argue further, but something in her tone convinced him to let the matter drop, at least for now.

Inside the gas station, a teenage girl with purple-streaked hair and multiple facial piercings stood behind the counter, rhythmically popping bubble gum while scrolling through her phone. She looked up with obvious interest when she saw their uniforms.

"You're here about Ben, aren't you?" she said without waiting for them to speak. "He's not really a drifter like everyone thinks. I mean, he drives this beat-up old Chevy pickup with a homemade camper shell on the back. I'm pretty sure he actually lives in that truck full-time."

"What makes you say that?" Shea asked, pulling out her small notebook.

"Well, he says he's just passing through on his way to 'here and there,'" the girl made air quotes with her fingers, "but he's been hanging around for weeks now. Plus, he asks way too many questions for someone who's supposedly just traveling through."

"What kind of questions?" Shea prompted, pen poised.

"Mostly about those dead girls everyone's talking about. About the lake and what happened there. It's weird though. It seems like he already knows most of the answers but wants to find out whether anyone else knows what he knows, if that makes sense." She blew a large bubble and popped it loudly. "Like he's testing people or something."

"Do you know where we might find Ben right now?"

The girl jerked her head toward the back of the building. "Sleeping behind the store, last I checked. He parks his truck back there most nights. The manager doesn't care as long as he buys stuff and doesn't cause trouble."

"Does he have a last name that you know of?"

"Nobody around here knows it. He just goes by Ben, says that's all anyone needs to know about him."

When Shea and Trevor walked around to the back of the gas station, they found a man in his fifties leaning against the side of a weathered pickup truck, smoking a cigarette. He had shoulder-length graying hair, several days' worth of stubble, and the kind of deep tan that came from spending most of his time outdoors. His clothes were clean but worn, and his boots had seen serious mileage.

"Ben?" Shea called out, displaying her badge prominently. "I'm Sheriff Callahan, and this is Deputy Bolton. We'd like to ask you a few questions if you don't mind."

The man took a long drag from his cigarette, studying them both carefully before dropping the butt and grinding it under the heel of his boot. "Does it really matter whether I mind or not?" His voice carried a resigned quality, as if he'd been expecting this conversation.

Shea drew a sharp breath through her nose, already sensing that this interview might be more challenging than anticipated. "We've had some serious incidents around here recently. Young women turning up dead. Word is that you've been asking questions about these cases. We'd like to know why."

Ben's weathered face broke into what might have been a smile, though it didn't reach his eyes. "Curiosity, mainly. Small towns are always the same, aren't they? Secrets rotting under the surface like worms waiting to be dug up by anyone smart enough to know where to look. Makes a person want to understand what's really going on beneath all the polite facades."

"What brought you to Misty Hollow this particular time?" Trevor asked, pulling out his notebook.

"Just passing through on my way north, like I told the girl inside. Thought I might hang around for a while, maybe do some fishing on that famous lake of yours. But you've got the whole area closed down now, don't you? Because of that last girl they found floating there." Ben's eyes narrowed slightly. "The one in the canoe."

Shea felt her blood chill. That specific detail about the canoe hadn't been released to the public. The official press release had only mentioned that a body had been discovered near the lake, without mentioning the positioning or the boat. "How exactly do you know about the canoe?"

The man shrugged with studied casualness. "I keep my ears open when I'm in towns like this. People talk, especially when they're scared. Information has a way of getting around."

"Sir, we're going to need you to come with us for formal questioning." Shea motioned for Trevor to prepare handcuffs. While they didn't have enough evidence to arrest Ben, it wouldn't hurt to bring him in and let him worry for a while about what they might know.

"No need for the restraints, Sheriff. I'll come along willingly." Ben held up his hands in a gesture of cooperation. "I've got nothing to hide from law enforcement."

Trevor backed off but remained alert as he led them to the patrol car and ushered Ben into the back seat. The drive to the station was conducted in tense silence, with Ben gazing out the window like a tourist taking in the sights rather than a potential suspect being brought in for questioning.

At the sheriff's office, Ben maintained his calm demeanor. However, Shea detected a trace of genuine worry flickering in his eyes when she activated the recording equipment in the interview room. The fluorescent lights cast harsh shadows on his lined face, making him appear older and more careworn than he did in natural sunlight.

"Please state your full name for the record," Shea began.

"Ben."

"Last name?"

He tugged nervously at his right earlobe, a gesture that suggested he was considering his response. "Wells. Ben Wells."

"Mr. Wells, we need to know about your knowledge of these murders. You mentioned details that haven't been made public." Shea leaned forward, studying his body language.

Ben crossed his arms defensively. "Look, I didn't hurt that girl—the Pearson girl or any of the others. I never laid a hand on any of them. However, I did see her that night. I saw her with someone else."

This revelation completely shifted the direction of the interrogation. Shea realized that Ben wasn't withholding information because he was guilty—he was hiding it because he didn't want to get involved in a murder investigation.

"Tell us exactly what you saw." Trevor's pen

poised over his notepad.

"There was a person dressed all in black, driving a dark SUV. They followed Abby when she left the gas station where she'd been meeting that boyfriend of hers. I thought it was kind of strange behavior, so I decided to follow them both and see what was going on."

"Abby was driving her own vehicle?" Shea asked. This was the first they'd heard about the girl having access to a car.

Ben nodded. "A little blue Honda sedan. Probably her parents' car that she'd borrowed for her secret meetings."

"Did you get a good look at the person following her?"

He shook his head. "Not really. They were wearing dark clothing and kept their distance, very professional about it. But I did manage to get a partial license plate number from the SUV. Tennessee plates, first three characters were 4DL."

Trevor jotted down this crucial information.

"If you thought this girl might be in danger, why didn't you intervene or call for help?"

"Because when they reached a T-intersection about two miles from the gas station, Abby turned left toward town and the SUV went right toward the lake. I figured whoever was following her had given up or lost interest." Ben's voice carried genuine regret. "If I'd known what was going to happen to her, I would have done something different."

Shea continued probing for additional details, but Ben's story remained consistent through multiple retellings. Without any concrete evidence linking him to the crimes, and with his information potentially helping their investigation, she thanked him for his cooperation and arranged for a deputy to drive him back to the gas station. Her instincts told her that Ben Wells wasn't their killer.

Back at Trevor's desk, Shea watched as he ran the partial license plate information through the state database. After several minutes of searching, he looked up with excitement.

"Got it. A black GMC Yukon registered in Tennessee to a David Blackwell of Knoxville. No apparent connections to Misty Hollow or anyone involved in this case." He paused, scrolling through additional information. "But here's something interesting—Mr. Blackwell reported his vehicle stolen from outside a church in Knoxville exactly two weeks before Abby Pearson's murder."

Shea felt her stomach twist with anticipation. "That timing is definitely not a coincidence. Keep digging into this connection."

After several more minutes of research, Trevor spoke again with growing excitement. "The church where the SUV was stolen—Riverside Baptist—hosted a regional peer mentorship retreat last spring. They brought in speakers from across the Southeast to discuss best practices and community outreach."

"Let me guess who delivered the keynote address," Shea said grimly.

"Marilyn Townsend. She spoke about 'Community Responsibility and Maintaining Moral Standards in an Immoral World.'" Trevor looked up from his computer screen. "According to the event program, she was there for three days, leading workshops and meeting with local youth leaders."

"We need to pay Mrs. Townsend another visit immediately."

When they arrived at the parsonage, a smiling and perfectly composed Marilyn answered the door as if she'd been expecting their visit. She wore a floral dress and had her hair arranged in an elaborate style that suggested she'd been preparing for some kind of social event.

"Sheriff Callahan, Deputy Bolton, what a pleasant surprise. How can I help you today?"

"We'd like to ask you about a retreat you led in Knoxville last spring," Shea said, watching the woman's face carefully for any reaction.

Marilyn nodded without hesitation. "Oh yes, that was several months ago. We partner with so many different organizations throughout the region that I sometimes have trouble keeping track of all our outreach efforts. Such wonderful, dedicated people at Riverside Baptist." She paused thoughtfully. "I do remember there was some excitement during our visit—Mr. Blackwell's vehicle was stolen from the church parking lot. Such a shame that things like that happen even at houses of worship these days."

"Do you think the theft might have had something to do with Abby Pearson's murder?"

Marilyn's expression didn't change, but there was something in her eyes—not fear or guilt, but something that looked almost like satisfaction or control. "I couldn't possibly speculate about such matters, Sheriff. That's your area of expertise, not mine."

"Would you like to come inside for some tea? I do so admire your perseverance in this investigation. What would our little town do without dedicated law enforcement officers like yourselves?" The words were pleasant enough, but behind them Shea caught that same glimmer of something unsettling—a sense that Marilyn was enjoying this verbal sparring match.

"Thank you for the offer, but we'll pass on the tea," Shea replied, forcing a polite smile. "We appreciate your time and cooperation."

As they walked back to their patrol car, everything about this case kept circling back to the pastor's wife. Marilyn had proximity to every victim through her various mentorship programs. She had gained their trust and learned their vulnerabilities, their schedules, their secrets. She knew exactly when and where these girls would be most vulnerable.

But despite all their suspicions, the sheriff's department still had nothing concrete they could take to a prosecutor. No fingerprints, no DNA evidence, no surveillance footage. Basically nothing but circumstantial connections and dead ends that any competent defense attorney could easily explain away.

"She's very good at this game," Trevor murmured as they drove away from the parsonage. "Almost too good. Something about this whole situation feels like she's not working alone."

He was echoing exactly what Shea had been thinking. "Maybe she has help, but I guarantee you that Marilyn Townsend is the mastermind behind these murders. Everything we've uncovered points directly back to her."

Back at the station, Shea's phone buzzed with an incoming text message. Her heart sank as she read the notification from dispatch. "We've got another missing girl. Betsy Jensen, age sixteen. She's a former participant in Marilyn's peer mentor program, and she was scheduled for a private counseling session with Marilyn yesterday afternoon—the same day she disappeared."

Trevor frowned as he absorbed this information. "That seems almost too obvious, don't you think? Why would Marilyn risk taking someone so directly connected to her programs?"

"We're definitely missing something important about how this operation works," Shea agreed. "How do you feel about conducting surveillance tonight? I think it's time we watched the Townsend house and see what happens after dark."

"I don't have any other plans," Trevor replied with a grin. "Count me in."

"Perfect. I'll pick you up at eleven-thirty. Make sure to bring drinks and snacks—we might be there for several hours."

It was nearly midnight when Shea parked their unmarked patrol car half a block down from the Townsend residence, positioning it behind a cluster of evergreen trees that provided natural camouflage. The old Victorian parsonage glowed with warm yellow lamplight from several windows, creating the impression of a peaceful, innocent household where nothing in the world could be wrong. The scene looked like something from a Norman Rockwell painting—the perfect picture of small-town American tranquility.

Shea knew better. In her experience, the most dangerous predators were often those who appeared most normal and trustworthy to their communities.

"Should we have brought backup for this operation?" Trevor asked quietly, handing her a bottle of water from their surveillance supplies.

"No, absolutely not. We can't risk having Marilyn realize she's being watched and potentially fleeing before we can gather concrete evidence." Shea checked her service weapon and made sure her radio was functioning properly. "Tonight, I need to be more than just the sheriff trying to solve a case. I need to become a hunter tracking dangerous prey."

She opened her door and motioned for Heidi to

join them, then moved silently through the darkness toward a cluster of juniper bushes that grew close enough to the house to provide an excellent observation point. Trevor crouched down beside her, both of them settling in for what might be a long night of watching and waiting.

Shea lifted her binoculars and focused them on the illuminated windows. A light was on in what appeared to be a corner room on the first floor, revealing floor-to-ceiling bookshelves and elegant furniture that suggested it was probably the pastor's study. Marilyn's distinctive silhouette moved back and forth across the window with graceful, deliberate movements that seemed almost choreographed.

On a table clearly visible through the window, something metallic caught the lamplight—a silver bracelet that Shea would bet her favorite boots belonged to the missing Betsy Jensen.

As Shea prepared to move closer for a better view, her radio suddenly crackled to life with an urgent message from dispatch.

"Sheriff, we've got a significant problem at the station."

"What kind of problem?" she whispered into the radio, not wanting to alert anyone in the house to their presence.

Deputy Butler's voice came through clearly. "Someone managed to breach our security system about twenty minutes ago. Our entire video surveillance network is down, and all the backup systems have been disabled. We also received an anonymous call reporting that Betsy Jensen's cell phone just pinged from a location near Misty Lake. The same general area where we found Abby Pearson's body."

Shea's mind raced as she processed this information. If Marilyn was visible inside her house, how could Betsy's phone be moving around the lake at this hour? The possibilities were troubling—either Betsy had somehow escaped and was trying to get help, or this was an elaborate distraction designed to pull law enforcement away from the real action.

Trevor tapped her shoulder urgently and pointed toward the back of the Townsend property.

A tall shadow had detached itself from the tree line and moved with obvious purpose toward a side entrance of the house. The figure wore dark clothing with a hood pulled up, making identification impossible in the dim moonlight.

Shea's fingers instinctively curled around her service weapon as she and Trevor began moving to intercept the mysterious visitor. They reached the side of the house just as the hooded figure reached for the door handle.

"Stop! Sheriff's department!" Shea commanded, her weapon drawn but not yet aimed directly at the suspect.

The figure spun around, and in the brief moment before they bolted, Shea caught a glimpse of what appeared to be a young man in his late twenties. His face was partially obscured by the hood, but she could see enough to know this wasn't anyone she recognized from their investigation.

The suspect immediately took off running across the backyard toward the dense woods that bordered the church property. Shea, Trevor, and Heidi gave chase, but their quarry had planned this escape route carefully. Within minutes, he had vanished completely into the darkness of the forest.

"He knew exactly where he was going," Trevor said, breathing heavily from the pursuit. "That wasn't random. He's familiar with this area and had an escape plan ready."

"Which suggests he's been here before, probably multiple times," Shea replied, calling Heidi back to her side. "An accomplice, maybe? Someone helping Marilyn with the logistics of these crimes?"

As they made their way back toward the house, Shea noticed that Marilyn now stood at the study window, still holding her steaming mug and watching them with obvious interest.

"You know exactly who he is, don't you?" Shea muttered under her breath, staring up at the illuminated figure behind the glass.

Marilyn raised her mug in what might have been a toast, and smiled down at them with an expression that seemed almost triumphant.

The psychological warfare had definitely escalated,

and Shea had the distinct feeling that their killer was just getting started with her games.

Chapter Ten

Shea woke the next morning to someone pounding insistently on her front door like they were trying to break it down. Heidi's deep barking echoed through the house, the German Shepherd's protective instincts fully activated by the urgent commotion. Shea's training kicked in immediately—she grabbed her service weapon from the nightstand drawer and padded on bare feet to the front window, carefully peering through the peephole while staying out of the potential line of fire.

Trevor stood on her front porch, his uniform rumpled and his hair disheveled as if he'd been running his hands through it repeatedly. His hand was raised to knock again when she opened the door. The familiar combination of urgency and frustration in his eyes meant they had another crisis on their hands.

"We've got another missing girl," he said without preamble, consulting a crumpled slip of paper in his hand. "Claire Smith, sixteen years old. But this time, Shea, we might actually have caught a break. There's a witness who saw something."

"Give me exactly two minutes." Shea left the door open for him to enter while she dashed to her bedroom to throw on clothes. She could hear him pacing in her living room, his boots clicking against the hardwood floors with nervous energy.

When she emerged, Trevor was already heading back toward his patrol car. "The witness is waiting for us at the station right now. She called in about an hour ago and insisted on speaking with us in person rather than giving her statement over the phone."

"How long has Claire been missing?" Shea asked, buckling her seatbelt as Trevor started the engine.

"Since last night around nine o'clock. She was supposed to be having pizza with friends at Tony's on Main Street, but she never showed up. Her parents didn't get worried until after midnight when she still wasn't answering her phone." He reached over and squeezed her hand briefly, a gesture of support that acknowledged the mounting pressure they were both feeling. "A witness, Shea. This could be the break that changes everything about this case."

If it's a reliable witness with accurate information. She'd seen too many investigations derailed by well-meaning but mistaken eyewitnesses. Still, it was more than they'd had before. "Let's hope so."

Mrs. Ira Tully was waiting in Interview Room B

when they arrived at the station. She was an elderly woman in her seventies with sharp, intelligent eyes and the kind of posture that suggested she'd been a schoolteacher or librarian in her younger days. She shot them both a penetrating look as they entered, clearly sizing them up.

"I saw that Pearson girl," she began without waiting for them to settle into their chairs. "The night before, they found her body floating in that boat. She was talking to someone—a man, I believe, though I couldn't get a clear look at him. He was sitting in an old dark green pickup truck parked near the phone booth by the drugstore."

Shea glanced at Trevor as she settled into the chair across from Mrs. Tully. This was the first they'd heard about a green pickup truck, and it didn't match the description of the dark SUV that Ben Wells had reported following Abby. "I'm sorry, Mrs. Tully, but I thought you were here to give us information about Claire Smith?"

"I am getting to that, Sheriff," the elderly woman said with a hint of impatience. "Don't rush me. These things are connected, and you need to understand the whole picture if you're going to catch this killer."

"You're absolutely right. Please continue."

"As I was saying, I saw Abby talking to whoever was in that truck. She leaned right into the driver's side window, real familiar-like, which told me she knew this person well. They weren't strangers." Mrs. Tully adjusted her glasses and fixed Shea with a stern look. "In my day, people used that old phone booth when they needed privacy for their conversations. Guess some things never change."

"Are you certain you saw a green pickup truck?" Shea asked, making detailed notes. This didn't match their previous witness accounts about dark SUVs.

"Sheriff, I may be old, but my eyesight is just fine, thank you very much. I know the difference between green and black, and I know a pickup truck when I see one."

"Of course. I apologize. What can you tell us about Claire Smith?"

"The same scenario, but with some differences. I saw Claire near that same phone booth yesterday evening around eight o'clock. She looked agitated, kept checking her watch like she was waiting for someone. But this time, I didn't see her talk to anyone in a vehicle. She used the phone booth itself, made what looked like a brief call, then walked away toward the lake."

Trevor looked up from his notetaking. "Did you see which direction she went after leaving the phone booth?"

"She headed down Lakeside Drive, toward the old camp area. Looked like she was in a hurry, almost like she was late for an appointment." Mrs. Tully leaned forward conspiratorially. "You might want to dust that phone booth for fingerprints. I have a feeling our killer has been using it to communicate with these girls."

It was an excellent suggestion. The phone booth would be an ideal way to contact potential victims without leaving a digital trail on cell phone records. "Thank you for that recommendation, Mrs. Tully. Is there anything else you remember that might be helpful?"

"Just that both girls seemed to know exactly who they were meeting. This wasn't random stranger danger—these girls trusted whoever was contacting them."

After Mrs. Tully left, Trevor immediately began running the license plate information for local green pickup trucks. Within an hour, he had a potential match.

"The truck is registered to Earl Wilson, age 58, local commercial fisherman," Trevor reported, reading from his computer screen. "He's got a minor criminal record—mostly bar fights and fishing without proper licenses. Nothing violent, but he's known to local law enforcement."

"Here's the interesting part," Trevor continued. "Earl reported his truck stolen exactly three days before Abby Pearson's murder. Same pattern we've seen with the other stolen vehicles."

"Let's pay Mr. Wilson a visit." Shea motioned for Heidi to follow them. "At this point, we can't afford to let any lead go uninvestigated, no matter how minor it might seem."

They found Earl Wilson at the public dock,

cleaning fish from his morning catch. He was a weathered man with calloused hands and the kind of deep tan that came from spending decades working outdoors. When they approached and identified themselves, he seemed more annoyed than concerned.

"Yeah, I heard my truck was seen around town," he said, continuing to clean his fish without looking up. "But it wasn't me driving it that night. Whoever stole it returned it two days later, parked right back where they took it from."

"Had you ever given Abby Pearson a ride before your truck was stolen?" Shea asked.

Earl nodded. "Once or twice, maybe. Sweet kid. She said she was meeting someone she didn't want her parents to know about. Figured it was probably some boy from school, and it wasn't my business to ask questions about teenage romance."

"Where exactly were you on the night Abby disappeared?" Trevor pressed.

"Playing poker at the VFW hall with about eight other guys. We meet every Thursday night." Earl grinned, revealing several missing teeth. "Don't tell anyone, though. Technically, gambling isn't legal in Misty Hollow."

Shea chose to ignore his admission of illegal gambling for now, and the fact he fished when the lake was supposed to be closed. Did no one follow orders in this town?

When Earl had nothing more substantial to offer

them, she informed him that they'd be verifying his alibi and requested that he not leave town without notifying their office.

Back in their patrol car, Shea turned to Trevor with a sense of growing urgency. "This case has gotten too big and too complex for our small department to handle alone. It's time to call in federal assistance."

Trevor nodded in agreement. "Most likely they'll send the same two agents who worked with us before—Agent Snowe and Agent Larson. Both of them are experienced with serial killer investigations."

"Good. I trust them to handle this professionally." Shea paused. "We might also want to consider enlisting some unofficial help. What do you think about asking the Misty Hollow Angels to assist with patrols?"

Trevor raised an eyebrow. "You mean the motorcycle club? That's an interesting idea."

"They know this town better than anyone, and they can cover ground faster than we can. Plus, they have a vested interest in keeping their community safe. Sometimes unconventional solutions work best."

Shea had just finished making the call to the FBI when her phone alerted her to an incoming text message. Claire Smith's cell phone had pinged from a location near the north shore of Misty Lake, approximately two miles from where they'd found Abby's body.

"That area is almost inaccessible," Trevor observed, studying the map coordinates. "It's all thick underbrush, briar patches, and fallen trees. No roads, just old deer trails."

"I'm not afraid of a few thorns and scratches," Shea replied grimly. "If that's where Claire is, that's where we're going."

The trek through the dense forest was grueling, with branches catching at their clothes and roots threatening to trip them with every step. But it didn't take long to locate Claire's phone—someone had deliberately placed it in the crook of an old oak tree about fifteen feet off the main deer trail, positioned where it would eventually be found but only after a thorough search.

Hanging from a branch directly above the phone was a silver necklace with a heart-shaped pendant engraved with the initials "C.S."—Claire Smith.

This was clearly a message from their killer, a taunt designed to show that they remained one step ahead of law enforcement. The killer was playing psychological games, demonstrating their control over the situation.

By the time Shea and Trevor returned to the station around noon, the FBI agents had already arrived and were setting up their equipment in the main conference room.

"We'd like to review all video surveillance footage you have," Agent Snowe said without wasting time on pleasantries. "Our technical team may be able to enhance images and extract information that your local equipment couldn't process."

"Anything you need," Shea replied. "Trevor, please bring them all the footage we've collected. Also, see if they can help us get our station's surveillance system back online after yesterday's cyber-attack."

"We'll definitely work on that," Agent Larson said, already booting up a sophisticated laptop computer. "Whoever sabotaged your system knew what they were doing, but we have some tools that might be able to restore the damaged files."

For the next five hours, the FBI team worked methodically through every piece of video evidence, using facial recognition software and enhancement programs that were far beyond the capabilities of the local sheriff's department. The conference room filled with the quiet sounds of computer keyboards and whispered consultations between the agents.

At exactly five o'clock, Agent Snowe called everyone together with obvious excitement. "We've managed to extract a clear facial identification from a camera near the church that apparently no one remembered was there. The system is so old and well-hidden that even the church staff may have forgotten about it."

She turned her laptop screen so that Shea and Trevor could see the enhanced image. "The facial recognition software identified him as Daniel Townsend, age 28. According to our database, he's Marilyn Townsend's nephew and has a history of minor psychiatric issues and drug-related arrests in Tennessee."

Shea felt pieces of the puzzle finally clicking into place. Marilyn Townsend wasn't working alone—she had enlisted her troubled nephew as an accomplice, possibly the one who actually carried out the physical aspects of the murders while she handled the psychological manipulation. Now all they needed was proof.

Within an hour, Shea and Trevor were once again standing on the front porch of the Townsend residence. This time, however, they weren't making a courtesy call.

"Mrs. Townsend, we have evidence that places your nephew Daniel at several of our crime scenes," Shea said bluntly. "We also believe you have in your possession jewelry that belonged to one of the murder victims."

Marilyn's expression didn't change by even a fraction. "Sheriff, those heart bracelets are sold by the dozens at the drugstore. I bought one to wear during our mentoring sessions—it helped me fit in with the girls, like a club badge or symbol of solidarity."

Out of the corner of her eye, Shea caught a glimpse of movement near the side of the house. Daniel Townsend was watching them from behind a large oak tree, clearly trying to remain hidden.

With a subtle movement of her head, she alerted Trevor to Daniel's presence. He nodded almost imperceptibly.

"Thank you for your time, Mrs. Townsend," Trevor said in a deliberately casual voice. "We appreciate your cooperation with our investigation."

They walked slowly back to their patrol car, pretending to be wrapping up their visit while actually preparing for pursuit. Just as they reached the vehicle, they heard the sound of a truck engine starting up behind the house.

Daniel Townsend's pickup truck came roaring around the corner, and he sped off in the direction of Misty Lake without bothering to check whether anyone was following him.

"Feel like another stakeout?" Shea asked, already reaching for her radio to coordinate with the FBI agents.

"Absolutely. This time we'll have proper backup and professional surveillance equipment."

Within thirty minutes, all four law enforcement officers had positioned themselves in concealed locations around the area where Abby Pearson's body had been discovered. Agents Snowe and Larson had brought night-vision cameras and motion sensors that would detect any approach to the shoreline.

Hours passed in tense silence. The night seemed to breathe around them, with normal forest sounds creating an eerie soundtrack to their vigil. Finally, around midnight, a hooded figure emerged from the tree line and began moving slowly toward the water's edge.

It was definitely Daniel Townsend, and he was carrying a large duffel bag slung over his shoulder along with what appeared to be a coil of rope in his other hand.

Shea waited until he was completely in the open with no escape route before making her move. "Freeze! Sheriff's department! Put your hands up where I can see them!"

Daniel started to run, but Trevor and the FBI agents had positioned themselves to box him in from all directions. Realizing he was surrounded, Daniel dropped the bag and slowly raised his hands in surrender.

"Where's Claire Smith?" Shea demanded, stepping closer with her weapon still drawn. "What has your aunt Marilyn instructed you to do with her?"

Daniel's lips twitched in what might have been the beginning of a smile. "Aunt Marilyn is a good, godly woman who's trying to save these girls from themselves. You're wasting your time investigating her."

"You need to see what's in this bag." Trevor had already opened the duffel bag and stared at its contents with a grim expression.

Shea peered inside. Her blood turned to ice. The bag contained dozens of silver heart bracelets identical to the ones found with each victim. There were candid photographs of all the murdered girls, apparently taken without their knowledge. Most disturbing of all was a small leather-bound notebook filled with names, dates, and coded notes written in a careful, methodical handwriting.

Scanning the names in the notebook, Shea's heart pounded as she realized the full scope of the killing operation. Claire Smith's name was there, along with dozens of others. Some names had been crossed out with red ink—these corresponded exactly to their known victims. A few names had gold stars next to them, possibly indicating girls who had "reformed" their behavior. But most chilling of all, there were at least twenty names that hadn't been marked at all—potential future victims.

Marilyn Townsend might be the mastermind behind these murders, the one who identified and selected the targets, but Daniel was clearly the enforcer—the one who actually committed the physical acts of killing.

"Where is Claire Smith?" Shea repeated, her voice carrying the full authority of someone who wouldn't accept evasion.

Daniel's expression turned genuinely cold as he looked directly into her eyes. "You're already too late, Sheriff. "

Chapter Eleven

The next morning, Shea took a breathing treatment on her nebulizer machine before pouring her first cup of coffee. The stress of the investigation had spurred another asthma attack. Thankfully, not severe enough to send her to the clinic.

When Trevor arrived to pick her up, his gaze fell on the machine. "You okay?"

"Better." She offered him a cup of coffee, which he declined.

"No, thanks. We've got to head to the lake. Claire's body has been found."

Shea took a deep, wheezing breath, then coughed, then exhaled slowly. She set her cup in the sink. "I'm ready."

The roar of motorcycle engines filled the air as they drove through town toward the lake. The Misty Hollow Angels were out in full force. Hopefully, their presence would deter the killer from abducting another girl.

When they arrived at the lake, the FBI agents were already questioning a man clutching a fishing pole like a lifeline. Shea asked the man to repeat what he'd found as her gaze darted toward a young girl lying on a plank of wood.

"I was fishing, same as always." A dart of fear flickered through his eyes. "Before you arrest me for fishing against your orders, just know that fishing is part of my livelihood, what with the price of groceries."

Shea waved for him to continue.

"Anyway, I thought maybe what I was seeing was a mannequin. A prank, but when it floated closer to shore, I knew it was the missing girl, Claire Smith. I'm right, ain't I?"

"Appears so." Shea moved to the girl's lifeless form. Her hair had been fanned out around her like moss, her eyes closed, hands folded across her chest. Just like the others. One silver star earring dangled from an ear. "Bruising around her wrists." She pointed out to Trevor. "Claire wasn't killed immediately. She'd been kept for a few hours at least. We need to find out where."

Trevor stepped closer to her. "Are you sure you're okay? You look a bit pale, and I don't think it's because of the crime scene."

"A little tightness in my chest. I've got my inhaler. I'll be okay." She patted his shoulder, warmed by his concern. Someday, maybe, she'd spend some time examining her growing feelings for him. In the middle of a murder investigation was not the time.

A crowd had gathered outside the sheriff's office when they arrived. Shouts rose as Shea exited the squad car.

"Is it Claire?"

"What are you doing to keep the girls of this town safe?"

"Enough is enough!"

Shea stopped on the top step and faced the crowd. "We have a suspect in custody. Rest assured that my department will not stop until the killer is brought to justice."

"What if you have the wrong person?" Someone asked.

"Then we'll keep looking." She shoved open the door and stepped inside the building before turning to Trevor. "If Daniel is the killer, he has help. He was locked up when Claire's body was placed at the lake."

"Marilyn."

"It does all seem to point to her. Keep digging into the Townsends' past. We're missing something. There has to be evidence against her or both of them." She headed to her office to rest and get her breathing under control.

After another breathing treatment with the nebulizer she kept in a cabinet in her office, she started digging into Marilyn's past. The woman had attended a private college in the northeast. Shea's eyes widened at the next sentence, and she rang for Trevor to join her.

"Find something?" He stood behind her, peering over her shoulder. The scent of his woodsy cologne filled her senses.

Shea tapped the computer screen. "Marilyn was briefly committed to a psychiatric facility after the death of her daughter. There is also a restraining order against Mark Townsend when he was a young preacher. Filed by a grieving mother who thought him responsible for the drowning of her daughter during a summer church camp. The case never went anywhere, but it sent the Townsends to Tennessee, then to Misty Hollow."

"I think we might finally be getting somewhere."

Shea nodded. "Marilyn's obsession with purity, perfection, and control over these young girls is more dangerous than we thought. She's punishing them for her own daughter's rebellion and death."

"I found something, too." He placed some printed-out pages on her desk. "Marilyn Townsend's aunt owned a private cabin near the lake. We missed it because it never transferred out of the aunt's name. I've already got a warrant in progress."

Shea shot him a smile. "Good job." She grabbed her jacket. "Come on, Heidi. We might need your nose."

It's nearly dusk when Shea and Trevor make their way through the dense woods to the northern edge of

Misty Lake. The FBI agents opted to stay behind to try and get more information out of the nephew.

A small, weathered cabin sat in the middle of a narrow clearing. Squat and gray with peeling siding and dark, shuttered windows. The front door is chained, but Trevor finds a side window open a few inches. He shoved it open and helped Shea through and into the house.

The smell of mildew and bleach assaulted her. She dug her inhaler out of her pocket and took two deep puffs.

Minimum furnishings filled the room. A table, two chairs, a cot. No personal effects, no dishes. Clearly, a hunter or fishing cabin.

She moved down a short hallway as Trevor landed inside with a thud. She froze in the doorway of a small room that had been converted into something that chilled her blood. On one wall were taped photos of young girls, some candid, some school photos. All of the girls were part of the mentorship program. Red yarn connected the pictures. This should be enough to bring the Townsends in for at least a twenty-four-hour hold.

"Found Claire's other earring." Trevor knelt in front of an old trunk.

Shea's breath caught. "So, she was held here."

"Yep, and there's more."

Inside, they found a set of printed papers—rules and lesson plans, written in a clinical, straightforward tone. At the top were the words "Moral Purity

Guidelines—Internal Use Only."

Shea scanned the documents, her stomach churning at the contents. The rules were detailed and disturbing, outlining proper behavior for "wayward girls" and the consequences for infractions. The lesson plans were worse—step-by-step instructions for breaking down a person's will and rebuilding them according to someone's twisted vision of purity.

"Trevor, look at this." She held up a page titled "Final Assessment Protocol." Her voice dropped to a whisper. "It's a manual for murder."

Trevor moved beside her, reading over her shoulder. "Listen to this: 'If the subject fails to demonstrate true spiritual transformation after all interventions, final purification may be necessary to ensure they do not corrupt others.'"

A chill ran down Shea's spine that had nothing to do with the cabin's damp air. "They're not just killing these girls randomly. They really believe they're saving them."

"And saving the community from them." Trevor flipped through more pages. "There are profiles here on each girl. Jennifer, Maria, Sandra, Claire. Look at what they wrote about a girl named Jennifer. She isn't one of the victims. Yet."

Shea read the neat handwriting in the margins. "Subject shows concerning attachment to worldly pleasures. Frequent attendance at school dances, inappropriate clothing choices, reports of kissing boys behind the gymnasium." She looked up at Trevor. "They were watching these girls for months."

"Building cases against them."

"Like some kind of moral court." Shea's radio crackled, interrupting her thoughts. She answered it while continuing to examine the papers.

"Sheriff, this is Wilson. We've got Daniel Townsend talking. You need to hear this."

"On our way." She keyed off the radio and looked at Trevor. "Let's see what Daniel has to say about all this."

Trevor gathered the evidence into a bag as Shea headed for the door. She froze.

Footsteps crunched outside. Shea and Trevor draw their weapons.

A figure moved past the window.

When Trevor dove out the window and leaped to his feet, the figure bolted into the woods. Shea quickly followed, but the person disappeared into the dark.

She holstered her weapon, breathing hard. The exertion combined with the stress was making her chest tight again. She pulled out her inhaler and took two quick puffs.

"You see who it was?" Trevor asked, brushing dirt off his jacket.

"Too dark. Medium height, moved fast. Could have been Marilyn, could have been someone else entirely." She looked back at the cabin, its windows now glowing with the flashlights of the approaching crime scene team. "Whoever it was, they know we found this place."

Frustrated, Shea radioed in what they'd found at the cabin so the crime scene techs could secure the property. Someone knew they'd be coming. Had been watching for them.

She waited with Trevor in front of the cabin until the crime scene team arrived. Flashing red and blue lights lit up the clearing like the Fourth of July. Shea paced, her jaw tight.

Trevor rubbed his arm. "Cut myself diving through the window." He rolled up his sleeve. "Just a scratch." He stopped Shea's pacing with a gentle hand on her arm. "We're getting there. We know Claire was here. This place belongs to Marilyn. All we have to do is go get her."

"It's not that simple." Shea pulled away, resuming her pacing. "Whoever ran from here tonight—they're going to warn anyone else involved. If it is Marilyn, she's already gone to ground. And if there are more people involved than just the Townsends..."

"You think there's a whole network?"

"I don't know what to think anymore." She gestured toward the cabin. "This level of organization, the detailed planning, the surveillance of these girls—it feels bigger than two grieving people acting out their trauma."

Agent Larson emerged from the woods, his flashlight beam cutting through the darkness. "Crime scene team's almost done with their initial sweep. They found something else you should see."

He led them to the back of the cabin, where technicians were photographing a small shed hidden behind overgrown bushes. The door hung open, revealing shelves lined with chemical containers.

"Cleaning supplies?" Shea asked.

"Some of them. But look at this." He pointed to a collection of bottles on the bottom shelf. "Industrial bleach, ammonia, and these." He indicated several unmarked containers. "The lab will have to confirm, but I'm betting these are drugs. Sedatives, maybe something to keep the victims compliant."

Trevor whistled low. "That explains how they controlled the girls without leaving defensive wounds."

"And the bleach explains why we've found so little forensic evidence on the bodies." Shea studied the shed's contents. "They've been perfecting this process."

"There's more." The agent led them around to the side of the shed, where someone had carved words into the weathered wood. "Look at this."

Shea shined her flashlight on the carving. The words "For Lily" were etched deep into the wood, with a date underneath: June 15, 2004.

"Lily Grossman," Trevor said quietly. "The girl who disappeared twenty years ago."

"But why would the Townsends care about Lily Grossman? They didn't even live here then."

Larson's radio squawked. He answered it, his

expression growing more serious with each exchange. When he signed off, he turned to Shea and Trevor.

"That was Agent Snowe back at the station. Daniel Townsend just confessed, but his story doesn't add up. He claims he and Marilyn killed all four girls, but he can't provide details that match the crime scenes. And here's the kicker—he says they did it because someone told them God wanted them to."

"Someone told them? Plus, there's more than four girls."

"That's the main thing that doesn't add up. He also keeps talking about 'the voice of righteousness' that guided them. Says this person showed them which girls needed to be saved and how to do it properly."

The pieces of the puzzle shifted in her mind, but the picture they formed was still unclear. "So, Daniel is obviously being used."

"That's what it looks like. And whoever's using him just watched us discover their base of operations."

The radio on her belt crackled. A sound she'd come to hate. "Sheriff Callahan."

"It's Butler. We've got another girl missing. Lily Davidson. No relation to the Grossman girl who disappeared so many years ago."

"Lots of girls are named Lily, Bill. Get a BOLO out for her and have Marilyn Townsend brought to the station. Start tracking Lily's phone. Now."

Shea bolted for the squad car. They didn't have a minute to waste. They were no longer one step behind the killer.

They were on the knife's edge.

Chapter Twelve

"What do you mean Marilyn is missing?" Shea stared at her phone.

"Exactly that, Sheriff." Deputy Butler sighed. "The pastor says he has no idea where his wife is. Hasn't seen her since last night."

If Shea was the swearing type, she would've let loose a string of expletives to singe ears. "Trevor and I are headed to the parsonage now." She hung up. Not only did they have another missing girl, but now their prime suspect had fled.

"Let's go wake up a pastor." Trevor sped toward the church.

The sanctuary door was locked. The stained-glass windows dull in the dim light of a clouded sky. The two of them moved to the back of the building where a light shined from a window.

Shea stepped back, hand on the weapon at her hip while Trevor knocked. Pastor Townsend, a cup of coffee in hand, answered the door and invited them in.

The parsonage felt oppressive, like the air itself was holding secrets. Dark wood paneling covered the walls, and religious artwork stared down at them from every surface. Crucifixes, paintings of Jesus, and framed Bible verses created a maze of moral judgment that made Shea's skin crawl.

As he poured two more cups of coffee, he said, "I guess you're here about my wife."

"Before we talk about her, I'd like to ask how well did you know the victims?" Shea tilted her head, declining the coffee, but taking a seat on a worn floral sofa. The fabric smelled of mothballs and disappointment. "Are you aware that Claire Smith's body has been found and your nephew, Daniel, in custody?"

"Yes." He sighed, settling into a leather chair that dominated the small living room. "I've been praying for all the families of the victims and...for my nephew."

"Do you know why we're here?"

Townsend's gaze locked with hers. Behind his wire-rimmed glasses, his eyes held a calculated calm that didn't match his words. "To pin something on me?"

Trevor glanced at his phone, then at the pastor. "I just received notice that you were one of the last known people to have spoken with Claire. She attended church on Sunday evening. Multiple people saw you walk her out."

Good going, FBI. Shea kept her face impassive

while studying Townsend's reaction. A muscle twitched in his jaw, and his fingers tightened around his coffee mug. "Claire never made it home. Where were you?"

"At home reading." His answer came too quickly, too rehearsed. "I'd say that Marilyn could verify my whereabouts, but she seems to have taken off."

"And why is that, Mr. Townsend?" Shea fought to keep her voice at a normal level. Her chest was tightening again, the stress of the case making her breathing shallow.

"I'm sure my wife is distraught over all that has happened. You do know about our daughter's death. This has brought all that grief to the surface. I'm sure once Marilyn has time to deal with her emotions, she'll return home."

The way he spoke about his wife's grief struck Shea as oddly detached, like he was discussing someone else's weather report. "Where would she go?"

"I don't know. I can promise you."

Right. If Shea was any judge of character at all, the man lied through his teeth. She glanced around the room, noting how sterile it felt despite the heavy religious décor. No family photos except for one formal portrait on the mantel—Mark and Marilyn standing stiffly beside a young girl who must have been their daughter. The girl's eyes held a sadness that seemed to reach across the years.

"Do you know where she kept the files on those who belonged to the Peer Mentorship program?"

He shook his head. "No, I'm sorry. That was all Marilyn. I'm kept busy enough with the church."

Trevor leaned forward. "Busy enough that you don't know what your wife does with teenage girls in your congregation?"

"The mentorship program has been a blessing to this community," Townsend said, his voice taking on the practiced cadence of a sermon. "Marilyn has helped dozens of young women find their way back to righteous living."

"Is that what you call it?" Shea pulled out her phone and showed him a crime scene photo. "Does this look like righteous living to you?"

Townsend barely glanced at the image of Claire's body before looking away. "I don't know what happened to those poor girls, Sheriff, but I can assure you my wife had nothing to do with their deaths."

"We've seen a necklace like the ones all the girls wore in your office, sir," Shea said, watching his face carefully.

Townsend's composure slipped for a moment. His eyes darted toward a closed door at the far end of the room before returning to Shea's face. "I do hope you don't plan on turning my wife into a monster based on a cheap piece of costume jewelry."

"May we see your office?"

"Not without a warrant." The friendly pastor mask was slipping, revealing something harder underneath. "I think this conversation is over."

Shea got to her feet, noting how Trevor positioned himself between her and Townsend. "You're right. We'll find out the truth, sir, with or without your help." She marched back outside, her breathing becoming more labored with each step.

Once they were back in the squad car, she pulled out her inhaler and took two deep puffs. "That man is hiding something."

"More than something. Did you see how he looked toward that office door when you mentioned the necklace?" Trevor started the engine. "We need that warrant."

"Already on it." Shea called Agent Wilson while Trevor drove back toward town. "We need a search warrant for the Townsend parsonage. Yes, I know it's a church. Just get it done."

By the next morning, the town buzzed with the news of Marilyn's disappearance. Some said the killer got to her, others said she was the killer, and the town became split in half. Multiple calls came into the station with sightings. Every woman in a hood became a suspect, every shadow in the woods became Marilyn Townsend.

The only viable lead was from a camera at a gas station in Langley, fifteen miles north of Misty Hollow.

Shea stared at the grainy footage on Butler's computer screen. A dark hoodie, sunglasses, a faded canvas backpack. The same shape as the person in the woods and the one they'd chased several times. The figure moved with purpose, head down, avoiding the camera's direct line of sight. Professional. Calculated.

She didn't use a credit card or speak to the clerk. Instead, she paid cash for a bottle of water and some protein bars, sliding the money across the counter without looking up. Even in the poor-quality footage, there was something unsettling about the deliberate way she moved.

"Marilyn Townsend's car has been found three blocks from the gas station behind an abandoned warehouse." Butler slapped a sheet of paper on Shea's desk. "The FBI located the car unlocked. Inside are these things." He started adding photographs to the list on the paper.

A well-worn Bible with highlighted passages, the pages soft from years of handling. Fast food trash—burger wrappers and empty fries containers that seemed oddly mundane given the circumstances. A church bulletin with notes scribbled on the back in Marilyn's neat handwriting. Her purse, empty except for a dried tube of lipstick and her driver's license.

The picture that caught Shea's attention the most was one of Claire Smith and Abby Pearson, smiling, arms around each other at what looked like a school event. They'd been circled with red ink, and someone had written "LOST" across their faces in the same red pen.

"There's more," Butler said, spreading additional photos across the desk. "A nearby farmer claims to have seen a woman cross his property right around sunrise. Said she looked like she knew where she was going. Didn't flinch a bit when the man's dog barked— big German Shepherd that usually scares off trespassers." Butler grinned. "There's a hunting cabin less than a mile from this farmer's property. Owned by some city folks who only use it during deer season."

Shea studied the map Butler had drawn, marking the gas station, the abandoned car, the farmer's property, and the cabin. The pattern suggested someone familiar with the area, someone who had planned this route in advance.

"Have we contacted the cabin owners?"

"Already did. They're in Florida for the winter, haven't been up here since October. But here's the interesting part—they said someone called them last month asking about renting the place. Woman's voice, said she was researching local history for a book."

Trevor joined them, carrying a fresh cup of coffee and looking like he hadn't slept. "Any word on Lily Davidson?"

"Phone's still dead. Last ping was near the mill district around midnight." Shea grabbed her jacket, wincing as the movement triggered a coughing fit. The stress was wreaking havoc on her respiratory system. "Come on, Heidi. We're taking a drive."

The hunting cabin stood nestled between pine and cedar trees, their branches heavy with morning frost. While the place had an air of being neglected—peeling paint, sagging porch steps, windows clouded with grime—the inside revealed that someone had stayed there recently.

A sleeping bag spread on the floor near the fireplace, wrappers from protein bars scattered on a wooden table, an empty water bottle, and footprints in the dust on the floor. The tracks were small, consistent with a woman's shoe size, and they led from the front door to every room in the cabin as if someone had been searching for something.

"She's been here, but not for long," Trevor observed, kneeling beside the sleeping bag. "Still warm. Maybe left this morning."

No sign of Marilyn now, though a page from a hymnal had been tacked to the wall above the makeshift bed. The paper was old, yellowed at the edges, and someone had highlighted a single verse with that same red ink they'd seen in the car.

"For nothing is hidden that will not be made manifest, nor is anything secret that will not be known and come to light." —Luke 8:17

"She's leaving us messages," Shea said, photographing the page with her phone. "This isn't random. She wants us to know something."

Trevor searched the rest of the cabin while Shea examined the hymnal page more closely. The handwriting in the margins was different from what they'd seen in Marilyn's files—shakier, more desperate. One word was written over and over in tiny script along the border: "Sarah."

"Who's Sarah?" Trevor asked, returning from the back room.

"I don't know, but we need to find out." Shea's radio crackled, and she answered it with growing dread.

"Sheriff, this is Wilson. We executed the warrant on the parsonage. You need to get back here now."

"What did you find?"

"Evidence. Lots of it. And something else—Pastor Townsend is gone."

No evidence that Lily Davidson or any of the other victims had ever set foot inside the hunting cabin, but the message on the wall suggested they were still missing pieces of a much larger puzzle.

~

Marilyn hadn't intended for things to go this far. The girls were supposed to get better under her tutelage. More pure, follow the rules. Listen to guidance instead of rushing headlong into sin and destruction like her own daughter had done.

She lit a candle and placed it beside the Bible she'd carried with her since her father gave it to her at sixteen. The leather cover was cracked now, held together with tape, but the words inside remained as powerful as ever. Highlighted in pink was the verse "Be sure your sin will find you out."

It had. Not only for her, but for all those girls. For her daughter Sarah.

Sarah, who had rejected everything Marilyn tried

to teach her about purity and righteousness. Sarah, who had run away at seventeen with a boy from school, pregnant and defiant. Sarah, who had died in that car crash three states away, her body found in a ditch with needle marks on her arms and shame written across her life like a scarlet letter.

She'd wanted the girls in the mentorship program to feel safe. That was the point—the mentoring, the retreats, the spiritual guidance. To save them from the fate that had claimed her daughter. Why hadn't they listened to her? All of this could have been avoided if they had just followed the rules, accepted the boundaries, embraced the purity she offered them.

Now, here she was in the middle of the woods because the sheriff and her deputy had discovered the lake cabin. She wrapped her arms around her bent knees as fog started shifting between the trees, making the morning light dim and uncertain.

Someone would find her eventually. Most likely Sheriff Callahan, who seemed determined to destroy everything Marilyn had worked to build. The woman had no understanding of what it meant to lose a child to the world's corruption, no appreciation for the careful work required to guide young souls away from temptation.

Marilyn needed a plan. She couldn't call her husband—Mark had always been weak when it came to difficult decisions. She couldn't contact Daniel—the boy was probably telling the authorities everything by now, too frightened to understand the righteousness of their mission.

She needed to find a better place to keep Lily Davidson, somewhere the authorities wouldn't think to look. She couldn't complete the girl's purification with the sheriff so close on her trail. The process required time, patience, the careful application of consequences until the subject understood the weight of their choices.

So many things to do. So many decisions.

Should she keep running, abandon the mission, leave Lily to face her sins alone? Or should she find a way to fix what she'd started, to complete the work that had been entrusted to her?

Marilyn opened her Bible to a random page, seeking guidance as she always did in times of crisis. Her finger landed on Matthew 18:6: "But whoever causes one of these little ones who believe in me to sin, it would be better for him to have a great millstone fastened around his neck and to be drowned in the depth of the sea."

The message was clear. The work must continue, no matter the cost. Lily Davidson and the others like her needed to be saved from themselves, even if that salvation came at the ultimate price.

Marilyn closed the Bible and blew out the candle. She had work to do.

Chapter Thirteen

The diner buzzed with news of Marilyn's disappearance. Shea sat in a booth, waiting for Trevor and staying alert in case things got physical and she had to intervene. The tension in the air was thick enough to cut with a knife, and her chest tightened with each raised voice.

"She's a cold-blooded killer!" Abby Pearson's mother stood nose-to-nose with another woman, her finger jabbing the air between them.

"Marilyn Townsend is a godly woman. The wife of our pastor." The other woman's face darkened, her church bulletin clutched in her white-knuckled fist. "You people are looking for a scapegoat."

"She lured our innocent girls to their death!" Tears poured down Mrs. Pearson's face, her voice breaking on each word. "My baby trusted her!"

Around the diner, other conversations had stopped. Everyone was listening, choosing sides, the divide in the community growing wider by the hour. Shea noticed how the booth sections had naturally segregated—church members on one side, grieving families and their supporters on the other.

"Things are really heating up." Trevor slid into the seat across from her, his jacket damp with morning drizzle. "And not just here at the diner."

"What do you mean?" Shea kept her voice low, aware of how many ears were straining to catch their conversation.

"There are photos tacked up all over town. Pictures of Marilyn with the victims. Some have Marilyn's face with a black X across it, others have the word Wanted printed across the top." He grabbed his menu but didn't look at it. "Someone even threw a rock through the stained-glass window of the church. The one with the Good Shepherd."

"Good grief." Shea rubbed her temples. A vigilante mob was the last thing they needed. "Any idea who's behind the posters?"

"Could be anyone. Half the town wants her head on a spike." Trevor glanced around the diner. "I've got a search party ready to head out in an hour, but we're going to have to be careful about who we let join."

"The Misty Hollow Angels?"

"Already patrolling the streets on their bikes. Making a hell of a racket, but no one has seen or heard from Marilyn. The woman seems to have vanished completely." He finally opened his menu, though Shea could tell his mind was elsewhere. "Butler's coordinating with the state police. They're sending a helicopter."

"Good. No one can stay hidden forever. We'll find her." Or she'd find them. Either way, Shea intended to make sure Marilyn spent the rest of her life behind bars.

"There's something else." Trevor leaned forward, lowering his voice even further. "Pastor Townsend has returned. No comment on where he went last night, but one of his neighbors saw him coming home around three in the morning. Muddy boots, torn jacket."

"We'll make time to question him again." Shea reached for her inhaler, taking a discreet puff as the stress continued to build in her chest. "After we check out those search areas."

The waitress approached their table, a middle-aged woman named Betty who'd been serving coffee at the diner for twenty years. Her usually cheerful demeanor was replaced by nervous energy.

"You folks deciding?" she asked, pencil poised over her order pad. "I've got to tell you, Sheriff, people are scared. Real scared. My granddaughter's the same age as those poor girls."

"We're going to find Marilyn, Betty. I promise you that."

Betty nodded, but worry lines creased her forehead. "Just... be careful out there. There's talk about folks taking matters into their own hands. Some of the men from the lumber mill were in here earlier, drinking coffee and talking about forming their own search party. They had rifles."

After Betty took their order and walked away, Trevor shook his head. "This is getting out of control fast."

"Then we better find her before someone else does."

After a quick breakfast of eggs and toast that Shea could barely taste, the two headed to the parking lot of the sheriff's office where a crowd of those wanting to hunt for Marilyn had gathered. More shouts of "string her up" and "make her pay" echoed across the asphalt.

Shea studied the faces in the crowd. Some she recognized—shop owners, farmers, parents of teenagers. Others were strangers, drawn by the media attention or their own dark curiosity. All of them united by anger and fear.

"We need to vet this group." Shea motioned for her deputies to mingle and remove those who seemed too radical to be of much help. "I don't want Marilyn killed. I want her to go to trial and all her sins exposed."

Deputy Butler approached a cluster of men near the back of the crowd, their voices carrying heated words about "justice" and "biblical punishment." She watched as he quietly suggested they might be more helpful manning roadblocks on the outskirts of town.

Agent Larson emerged from the building, his expression grim. "Sheriff, we need to talk. Privately."

Inside her office, Wilson closed the door and

turned to face her and Trevor. "We got the lab results back from the hunting cabin. The DNA on that sleeping bag belongs to Marilyn Townsend, as expected. But we also found traces of chloroform and something else—scopolamine."

"Devil's breath," Trevor said quietly. "That would explain how she controlled the victims without leaving defensive wounds."

"There's more. We found Lily Davidson's phone." Wilson placed an evidence bag on Shea's desk. "It was in a trash can three blocks from the church. Someone wanted it found."

Shea stared at the cracked phone screen. "She's playing games with us."

"That's what I'm thinking. This whole thing feels choreographed, like she wants us to follow a specific trail."

It took another hour to get a group of searchers Shea felt capable of doing the job without resorting to frontier justice. She assigned a deputy to each group and a map of the specific area they were responsible for covering. She and Trevor would continue with their search around the hunting cabin.

The crowd dispersed with reluctant grumbles, some heading home, others joining the official search parties. Shea noticed several of the more aggressive voices weren't among any of the groups—they'd simply melted away, which worried her more than if they'd stayed.

Fatigue settled on Shea's shoulders as she trudged through the dark woods with Heidi at her side and Trevor a few feet away. Although they searched in broad daylight, the canopy of pine and oak blocked most of the sunlight, creating an almost twilight atmosphere even at midday. This case had stretched her thinner than any she'd worked on before.

Sure, she could delegate more to her deputies, but she felt the need to investigate each lead personally. Too much was at stake, too many lives hanging in the balance.

"Footprints." Trevor knelt near an aging oak tree, brushing aside fallen leaves. "Fresh. Not more than a day old. Size seven, maybe eight. Could be our girl."

Shea headed his way, Heidi sniffing at the disturbed earth, then stopped as a sound cut through the forest. A woman's voice, singing Amazing Grace in a clear, haunting tone that seemed to come from everywhere and nowhere at once. Marilyn.

She put a hand on Heidi's head to keep her quiet and headed toward the sound, her weapon drawn and ready. The melody was beautiful and terrible, a hymn turned into something twisted by the circumstances.

As she crested a small hill, the singing stopped abruptly. No sign of anyone. No movement in the small mountain meadow spread out below them. Just wildflowers swaying in the breeze and the distant sound of running water.

"I didn't imagine it."

"No, you didn't." Trevor shook his head, his own weapon ready. "I heard her, too. She could be luring us into a trap."

"Let her. We won't be caught unaware." She led the way down the hill and into the meadow full of wildflowers—Indian paintbrush, wild lupine, and mountain laurel, creating a carpet of color that seemed obscene given the circumstances.

A sheet of paper waved from the branch of a maple tree at the far edge of the meadow, moving like a white flag of surrender. Shea snapped a glove over her right hand and pulled it free, noting how it had been deliberately placed at eye level, impossible to miss.

Damp and weathered, the edges starting to curl, the half of a page definitely came from Abby Pearson's diary. Shea recognized the handwriting—the careful cursive she'd seen in the school files. "He told me I was special. That I was different from the others. I believe him. I love him."

"Do you think she confided her feelings to Marilyn?" Trevor read over Shea's shoulder, his breath warm against her neck. "Could be why Marilyn thought she was breaking the rules. She was sneaking off to meet some young man."

"Could be." Shea folded the page and slipped it into her pocket, but something nagged at her. The handwriting looked familiar in a way that went beyond the school files.

Why all the way out here? They strongly suspected

Marilyn had been sleeping in the hunting cabin. She'd obviously had her hands on Abby's diary at some point. Why hang this page on a tree in the middle of nowhere? To gloat? To taunt? To lure them deeper into the woods?

She glanced at Heidi, who sniffed around the clearing with increasing excitement. The dog gave a single sharp bark, then bounded toward the left side of the meadow. Shea and Trevor followed until a creek blocked their way, the water running fast and cold from recent mountain rains.

Despite the dog pacing up and down the creek bank, whining and pawing at the muddy shore, she didn't catch the scent again. Whatever trail they'd been following ended at the water's edge.

"She crossed here," Trevor said, studying the far bank. "Probably waded downstream to throw off the scent."

"Smart. And she knows these woods better than we thought." Shea pulled out her radio. "All units, we need boats on Miller's Creek. Suspect may have used the waterway to evade detection."

They continued searching well past the lunch hour and close to suppertime, finding two more pages from what appeared to be different diaries—fragments of teenage thoughts and fears that Marilyn had turned into evidence of corruption. Each page was placed deliberately, leading them deeper into the wilderness and further from any meaningful leads.

Back in town, more people had gathered in front of the sheriff's office, their numbers swollen by curiosity seekers and media personnel. The crowd had taken on an uglier edge as the day wore on, prompting Shea to drive to the back entrance and slip inside through the employee door.

Inside, Doris, the receptionist, rushed toward them, her usually perfect hair disheveled and her face flushed with stress.

"It's a madhouse out there. Folks are demanding you do something. Most aren't sending their daughters to school anymore. Not until Marilyn is caught." Doris took a deep breath, her hands shaking slightly. "The mayor called three times, and there are reporters from Nashville and Memphis wanting interviews. Do you really think she's the killer?"

"Yes. Don't let anyone but law enforcement inside. Are the agents here?"

"In the conference room. They came up as empty as you did, but they found something else." Doris lowered her voice. "Another body. Not here—two counties over. Similar signature, but different enough to lead us to believe we have a copycat."

Shea's blood ran cold. "When?"

"This morning. Local sheriff called it in an hour ago."

"Thank you." Shea and Trevor headed to join the agents, the weight of another victim pressing down on her like a physical force.

~

The woods were chilly at night, even in late spring. Marilyn crouched between two massive boulders, hunkering in a slight overhang that provided shelter from both the wind and prying eyes. She pulled a tattered wool blanket tight around her shoulders, the fabric scratchy against her skin but warm enough to stave off hypothermia.

She couldn't risk a fire. The sheriff and her deputy had passed just feet from her hiding spot on the other side of the creek, their voices carrying clearly across the water.

She clutched her backpack tight against her chest, inventory taking of her meager supplies. All she had to sustain her was a half-empty water bottle, one protein bar, and half a sheet of paper from Abby's diary. She'd left the other half for the sheriff to find, a breadcrumb trail to show the woman that Marilyn stayed two steps ahead of her.

"Who had she loved?" Marilyn whispered to herself, her breath forming small clouds in the cold air. "That boy who lived behind the gas station? The one with the motorcycle and the cigarettes? Surely, I taught her better than that."

Nevertheless, the girl had disobeyed. Had chosen lust over purity, sin over salvation. Her cleansing had been necessary to save her soul from eternal damnation.

Same as with the other girls. Oh, how she missed them all. Sweet and innocent—until they weren't. Until the world corrupted them with its false promises and empty pleasures.

Tears trickled down her cheeks in a rare moment of weakness. The whole town must think her a monster. They didn't understand her mission to save the young women of Misty Hollow from an eternity in hell. They couldn't see past their grief to recognize the mercy she had shown their daughters.

She started humming Amazing Grace again, softer this time in case a search party still patrolled the woods after dark. She'd heard them talk about justice being served, but their version of justice was earthly and flawed.

She wasn't hiding to escape justice. She hid because justice no longer knew her name.

Chapter Fourteen

Butler rushed into the conference room, his boots clicking against the linoleum floor with urgency. "Got something, Sheriff." He set a pair of shoes on the table with a satisfied thud.

Shea frowned, leaning forward to examine them. "Who do those belong to?"

"The pastor." Butler grinned, unable to contain his excitement. "I found them outside the back door of the church, tucked behind a trash can like someone was trying to hide them. Noticed pollen on them—unusual stuff, not the regular kind you'd find around town."

Trevor picked up one of the shoes, a well-worn brown oxford with mud caked around the sole. "Looks like someone's been doing some hiking."

"Now, I've lived in Misty Hollow my whole life," Butler continued, "and there are only a few remote places this type of pollen can be found. My grandfather used to be a beekeeper, taught me about different pollens when I was a kid. This particular stuff—it's from mountain laurel and wild azalea that only grows in specific microclimates." He pointed to the yellowish dust coating the leather. "One of them is near the hunting cabin the pastor's wife hid in."

"Thank God for your great instincts." A rare grin spread across Shea's face, the first genuine smile she'd managed in days. "I owe you a beer, Deputy."

"More than one, I'm thinking." He chuckled and gave a mock salute. "Let me know if I can use this wonderful brain of mine to do anything else for you."

"Go sit down before that big head of yours explodes." Trevor laughed, but his expression quickly turned serious. "This proves Townsend's been lying to us."

After a few more minutes of good-natured ribbing that helped ease the tension in the room, Shea turned everyone back to the job at hand. The FBI agents had been studying topographical maps spread across the conference table, marking potential hiding spots and escape routes.

"I'd like to put a couple of game cams by the church," Shea announced. "See where our dear pastor gets off to at night. He knows where Marilyn is. I guarantee you."

Agent Wilson looked up from the maps. "We can have surveillance equipment in place within the hour. Motion-activated, infrared capable."

"Good. And I want someone watching the live feed

at all times. If Townsend so much as steps outside to get his mail, I want to know about it."

They didn't see anything on the cameras the first night. Townsend appeared to follow his normal routine—lights out by ten, no movement until morning prayers at six. But Shea had a feeling he was being cautious, waiting for them to lower their guard.

The next night proved her instincts correct. Around 1 a.m., Townsend exited through a side door of the church, moving with the practiced stealth of someone who'd done this many times before. He climbed into a dark sedan parked in the shadows behind the building.

He didn't turn on his headlights until he left the church parking lot, driving slowly through the sleeping town like a man with secrets to keep.

"Got him," Trevor whispered into his radio as they watched from their position across the street. "He's heading north on Pine Street."

"Roger that," came Agent Snowe's voice through their earpieces. "We'll track him as far as we can without being spotted."

But Shea had a different plan. "Let him go. We'll be waiting when he gets back."

Shea and Trevor slipped into the church through the same side door Townsend had used, their flashlights cutting through the darkness of the sanctuary. The sanctuary felt hushed, heavy with the weight of years of prayers and confessions. Moonlight shined through the stained-glass windows, minus the one that had been broken and boarded up with plywood. The broken window seemed like a wound in the building's facade, a visible sign of the community's fracturing faith.

While they waited, Shea stared at the cross on the wall behind the podium. It was a simple wooden cross, nothing ornate or expensive, but it dominated the space with its presence. How could two people who professed to love God, people who said they cared about the souls of Misty Hollow, turn into killers? What kind of twisted logic allowed them to justify murder in the name of salvation?

"He's here," Trevor said from his stance by the front door, his voice barely above a whisper. "Headlights just turned into the parking lot. He's heading for the parsonage."

"Let's go have a chat." Shea stood, cast one more glance at the cross—wondering if it would bear witness to a confession tonight—then followed Trevor across the empty parking lot.

The parsonage windows glowed with warm yellow light, making it look deceptively cozy and innocent. Shea knocked firmly on the front door, not bothering with the polite tap of a social call.

"Mr. Townsend." Shea stepped inside once he opened the door, not waiting for him to extend an invitation.

"Sheriff. Deputy." Surprise and maybe fear flickered in his eyes. He was still fully dressed despite the late hour, his jacket slightly damp from the night air. "Something wrong? I don't usually get visitors this late at night."

Shea closed the door behind them with a deliberate click. Trevor positioned himself near a bookshelf filled with religious texts and family photos, arms crossed, blocking any potential escape route to the back of the house.

"Where were you Wednesday night?" Shea pulled up a chair from the dining table and motioned for the pastor to have a seat on the sofa.

The man blinked rapidly, his hands fidgeting with the hem of his jacket. "Here. I had some prayer requests to get through. Wednesday night is always busy with—"

"Try again." Shea didn't break eye contact as she showed him a photo printed from a CCTV camera on Main Street. The image was grainy but clear enough to show his sedan driving through town at 1:17 a.m.

Townsend's shoulders sagged slightly. "I needed air. The deaths of these girls is almost too much to bear. Sometimes I drive around town, praying for the families, asking God for guidance."

Trevor stepped forward, pulling out his phone to show another image. "We found pollen on a pair of men's shoes that were discovered outside the church. The pollen is only found in one place around here—the remote area near the cabin where Marilyn hid." He showed him a picture of the shoes. "I've seen you wear these shoes, Mr. Townsend. Every Sunday for the past month."

"You've been visiting your wife, haven't you?" Shea leaned forward, her voice taking on the edge she used with suspects who were running out of lies. "Taking her food and water. Supplies. You're harboring a fugitive, sir. I'm starting to believe that maybe you had a hand in the murder of all those girls."

His composure started to crack like ice under pressure. He rubbed both hands roughly over his face, and when he looked up again, his eyes were red-rimmed and hollow. "She wasn't always like this."

"Tell us the truth. All of it, or we take you to the station in handcuffs." Shea's patience was wearing thin. Every minute they spent here was another minute Lily Davidson might be suffering.

He clasped his hands in his lap hard enough to turn his knuckles white. "I found out two years ago. Marilyn had been sneaking out at night, coming home with mud on her clothes, her hair wet and smelling like lake water. I thought maybe she was having an affair, so I followed her one night."

Trevor frowned. "Where did she go?"

"I kept a safe distance behind her with my lights off, parked about a quarter mile away and followed on foot." His voice dropped to almost a whisper. "Instead of meeting another man, she headed for the lake alone. By the time I caught up to her, she was soaked and covered in mud, dragging something heavy toward the water."

Shea's stomach turned. "What was she dragging?"

"When I asked her what she was doing swimming fully clothed at that time of the night, she said, 'She wouldn't stop crying.'" He shook his head, the memory clearly haunting him. "I didn't understand at first. Then I saw the bundle she'd been pulling—it was wrapped in a blanket, about the size of a person."

Trevor cleared his throat. "Who was it?"

"One of the girls in the program. I don't know her name. Like I said, the program was all Marilyn's domain." His face crumpled. "I should have called the police right then, but she is my wife. She looked at me with such conviction, such certainty that what she'd done was right."

Shea's voice turned ice-cold. "Why didn't you report this?"

His face fell, aging him ten years in as many seconds. "I tried to talk her into turning herself in. She refused. Said I wouldn't understand, that what she was doing wasn't murder—it was mercy. That she was saving these girls from a life of sin and corruption." He looked up at them with haunted eyes. "That told me she'd killed before. Maybe many times before."

Trevor stepped closer, his voice hard. "So, you let her keep on killing."

Tears sprang to Townsend's eyes, the first genuine emotion he'd shown all evening. "I tried to stop her. Begged her, threatened to leave her, but I didn't know what she'd done until it was too late. I didn't know how many times she'd killed, how long this had been going on." His voice broke. "She truly believes she's helping them. In her mind, she's sending them to heaven pure and unmarked by the world's corruption. The death of our daughter warped her."

"The nephew?" Shea forced the question from a throat tight with disgust. "Daniel?"

"He's simply an errand boy. Marilyn convinced him that they were helping troubled girls find their way back to God. She's very persuasive when she wants to be." He lowered his head, unable to meet their eycs. "Although I do believe he's recently discovered what Marilyn is really up to. The boy's been asking questions, acting nervous."

The room fell silent for several minutes, the weight of Townsend's confession settling over them like a shroud. Outside, a clock somewhere in town chimed three times, marking another hour closer to dawn.

Finally, Shea spoke again, her voice carrying the authority of someone who'd heard enough. "You are going to help us bring her in. No more secrets. No more lies. And when this is over, you will resign as pastor of my town."

He nodded, the fight gone out of him completely.

"Good. No more sneaking out. Do not leave town. Do not contact your wife. We'll be in contact within twenty-four hours with a plan. Only then will you send Marilyn a message." Shea stood and marched from the man's home, Trevor close behind her.

The next morning, Shea, Trevor, the FBI agents, and Deputy Butler gathered around the table in the conference room. Coffee cups and case files covered every surface, and the air was thick with cigarette smoke from Agent Wilson's chain-smoking habit.

Shea glanced at each face at the table, noting the fatigue and determination in equal measure. "Mark Townsend confirmed what we already suspected. That his wife is the killer. He's been protecting her for two years, watching her murder young girls and doing nothing to stop it."

Agent Wilson leaned forward. "What about the nephew?"

"According to Townsend, Daniel recently found out but has had no part in the actual killings. He's been manipulated, used as muscle and an errand boy."

Butler shook his head, disgust evident in his voice. "A church leader covering for his wife. Those girls could've been stopped years ago if he'd done the right thing."

"Now, it's up to us to stop her." Shea took a deep breath, relieved her lungs didn't wheeze for the first time in days. "Marilyn is hiding somewhere close. Since we haven't located Lily Davidson's body, I'm going to say the girl is still alive. Marilyn's keeping her somewhere, maybe trying to 'save' her before..."

She didn't finish the thought. They all knew how it would end if they didn't find Lily soon.

Doris entered the room and set a folded piece of

paper in front of Shea. "Sorry to interrupt, but this looks important. It's from the pastor. He said it was urgent."

Shea unfolded the note and read it out loud. "Townsend remembers one time after moving to Misty Hollow that his wife took some time off and stayed in a rented tiny house on the far side of the lake. Said she needed space to pray and reflect, but now he thinks she was scouting locations." She met Trevor's gaze. "We've got her."

He nodded but looked concerned. "Unless he alerts her and she runs."

"I don't think he will. I believe the man is ready for this to all be over. The guilt's been eating him alive." Shea spread out a detailed map of the lake area. "I've got a plan."

She pointed to different locations on the map. "Agent Snow and Larson will enter from the east path, here. Trevor and I will take the west approach. Butler, I want you in a boat on the water with backup, cutting off any escape by lake."

Butler crossed his arms. "What about Townsend?"

"Mr. Townsend will wear a wire and lead us straight to his wife. We go on foot. No cruisers. No lights. No radios until we're in position."

Butler frowned. "I still say her husband will tip her off. What if the woman is armed? We could get into a shootout and that girl could wind up dead like the others."

Trevor spoke up. "She's unstable. I agree that if she

thinks this is the end, she may turn violent. Could even kill Lily out of spite."

"I understand the risks, but this is the best chance we've got. I want her brought in alive if possible." Shea's voice carried finality.

The others nodded grimly. They all knew the stakes when a cornered killer had nothing left to lose.

"We move at dawn. Trevor and I will make sure Townsend meets up with her at seven a.m. He'll lead her to a clearing where we'll all converge. Stay hidden. Stay quiet. Don't hesitate to shoot to wound if she tries to bolt." Shea looked each person in the eye. "Again, I want her brought in alive. But not at the cost of Lily Davidson's life."

~

Marilyn sat on the edge of the narrow cot in the tiny house she'd rented under an alias three months ago. The place was barely larger than a shed—one room with a kitchenette, a fold-out bed, and a single window that looked out over the dark water of Misty Lake.

A single oil lamp flickered in the corner, casting dancing shadows against the pinewood walls. Outside, the wind moaned through the trees, making the small structure creak and sway slightly. The sound used to be comforting, like being rocked to sleep, but now it felt ominous.

She used to pray in moments like this, but the silence no longer felt peaceful. Instead, it threatened to suffocate her. God's voice, once so clear and guiding, had become muddled with doubt and fear.

She stared at the text message on the burner phone in her hand, reading it for the fourth time. "Meet at the clearing at seven. Miss you. Need to see you."

Mark's words felt wrong, false. He'd seen her just three nights ago when he'd brought supplies—canned food, bottled water, and news from town. His lie tasted sour even through the digital text.

Knowing that her husband had likely betrayed her didn't surprise her as much as it should have. Oh, she wasn't foolish enough to think the sheriff wouldn't be waiting at the clearing. No, Mark had finally chosen the world's version of justice over God's plan. He was as blind as the rest of the town to the holy work she'd been called to do.

Dying didn't scare her, nor was she afraid of the town's judgment. She'd made peace with her mortality long ago, when Bella had died. Death was just another doorway, and she'd already sent so many pure souls through it ahead of her.

She stood and paced the small area, her footsteps echoing off the thin walls. From a manila envelope on the tiny table, she lifted a photo of a smiling Abby Pearson. The girl who reminded her the most of her daughter—the same defiant spark in her eyes, the same willful spirit that needed gentle correction.

She ran her finger over the photo, tracing the outline of Abby's face. "You wanted out. You thought you were strong enough to get away from what you'd become. You weren't." Her voice was soft, almost maternal. "But I helped you find peace, didn't I? I made sure you were pure when you met your maker."

Tomorrow, she'd meet Mark in the clearing at seven and put an end to it all. But first, she had one more soul to purify. Lily Davidson was still tied up in a cave in the woods.

Tomorrow would be the end.

Chapter Fifteen

Shea and Trevor followed Townsend to the edge of the clearing fifteen minutes to seven. The morning air was crisp, carrying the scent of pine and damp earth. Fog clung to the low places, making the entire scene feel ethereal and dangerous.

As the man stepped out to wait for his wife, they hunkered down in some thick foliage, the dew soaking through their pants. Shea checked her weapon one more time, her breathing already showing signs of stress-induced tightness. The agents were positioned across the clearing, invisible among the trees.

Marilyn also arrived early, stepping from behind a cluster of pine trees like a specter emerging from a nightmare. The woman looked disheveled, pale, with eyes rimmed with red from sleepless nights and mounting desperation. Her clothes hung loose on her frame, suggesting she'd lost weight during her time in hiding.

She used Lily as a shield, holding a gun to the girl's head with one arm while keeping the teenager pressed tight against her body. Lily's face was streaked with tears and dirt, her eyes wide with terror.

"Step aside, traitor." She glared at Mark with venom that could have melted steel. "As for the sheriff and the deputy, I know they're here. Come out. Now, or I shoot this girl right here."

Shea glanced at Trevor who shook his head frantically. "She'll shoot you the moment you show yourself."

"Better me than the girl." Shea's voice was barely a whisper. She could feel her chest beginning to constrict, the familiar warning signs of an impending attack.

"Shea, I have a shot," came Agent Wilson's voice through her earpiece.

"No, Trevor. We can't risk Lily being harmed." She made the decision that would haunt her for the rest of her life—however long that might be. She stepped out with her hands up, moving slowly and deliberately.

"Aren't you the clever one," Marilyn sang, her voice taking on an almost childlike quality that was more terrifying than outright rage. She shot a look at her husband who slowly backed toward the trees, his face a mask of shame and terror. She shrugged, obviously deciding he wasn't worth her time or ammunition.

"What do you want?" Shea's chest tightened with

each word.

"I want you to come with me and Lily, or she dies." Marilyn's grip on the gun was steady, professional. This wasn't the trembling hand of an amateur—she'd done this before.

"No." Trevor's voice cracked as he stepped from his hiding place, unable to stay concealed while watching Shea walk into certain death.

"Stay back." Shea's voice trembled as she whispered urgently. "I need you to come find us. Promise me."

"I promise," he said, though the words felt like glass in his throat.

"Come on, Sheriff. Let's finish this." Marilyn kept Lily in front of her as she backed toward the deeper woods. "We have so much to discuss about God's plan for this town."

Shea's lungs tightened like a vise. Her vision began to narrow at the edges, the first sign of oxygen deprivation. No. Not now. She pressed a hand to her chest, fighting to keep her breathing steady.

"Shea?" Trevor made an involuntary move toward her, every instinct screaming to help.

"My inhaler." Shea slipped her hand into her pocket, fingers closing around the familiar plastic device. Before she could bring it to her lips, Marilyn's sharp voice cut through the air.

"Drop it. Now."

"Why?" Trevor demanded, his weapon trained on

Marilyn but unable to take a shot with Lily in the way. "She needs it to breathe."

"If she can't breathe, she can't fight." Marilyn moved closer to the tree line, dragging Lily with her. "Come on, Sheriff. We don't have all day. I know the FBI is waiting to take a shot at me the moment they have a clear line."

"Let...me...go." Shea's words came out in short bursts as she followed Marilyn, the inhaler falling from her fingers to land in the wet grass.

"I can't!" Trevor's anguish was evident in every syllable.

"You have...to." Her voice was barely audible even to her own ears. Shea cast one last look at Trevor—memorizing his face, the concern in his eyes, the way his hair fell across his forehead—then took a stumbling step forward.

As she followed Marilyn deeper into the woods, her breath grew shallower with each step. She focused on taking as deep a breath as her constricted airways would allow and willed herself not to pass out. She'd walked into a trap, but it was the only way to maybe save Lily Davidson's life.

Branches clawed at Shea's arms and tangled in her hair as she forced herself to stay upright and follow Marilyn through the increasingly dense forest. Above them, the sky turned pewter gray, promising rain that would wash away any tracks Trevor might follow.

"Stop," Lily begged, her voice hoarse from

crying. "The sheriff needs her inhaler. Please, you said you wanted to help people."

"I don't care," Marilyn snapped, but something in her voice suggested otherwise. "It won't matter soon anyway."

Every breath Shea took was a battle against her own body. Each inhale wheezed through clenched airways. Her legs threatened to give way beneath her, muscles weakening as oxygen deprivation set in. Still, she forced herself to continue, one foot in front of the other.

The path wound deeper into the forest, away from any chance of quick rescue. Marilyn seemed to know exactly where she was going, taking turns that led them further from civilization. How long had she been planning this? How many escape routes had she memorized?

Marilyn suddenly veered off the main path and onto a narrow deer trail barely visible through the undergrowth. Shea tried to follow and tripped on a gnarled tree root that jutted up from the forest floor. A gasp tore from her throat as she fell hard to her knees, palms scraping against rough bark.

"Get up." Marilyn sneered, replacing the gun with a long-bladed knife she'd retrieved from a sheath hidden in the pocket of her loose-fitting sweater. The blade caught what little light filtered through the canopy. "I'd rather not shoot or stab either of you. Water is what we need. You can't die here—not yet."

"I'm…going…to." The words came out between desperate attempts to draw air.

Marilyn frowned, and something flickered across her face. Doubt? Remorse? For a moment, she looked less like a cold-blooded killer and more like the church woman she'd once been. "You're not dying here. Get up." She held the knife closer to Lily's throat, a thin line of blood appearing where the blade kissed skin.

The woman gestured toward a crude shack next to a babbling stream, barely visible through a stand of birch trees. The structure looked like it had been abandoned for years—rotting logs, a collapsed corner, holes in what remained of the roof. A blue tarp was spread next to the water's edge.

"Sit there." Marilyn pointed to the tarp with the knife.

"I can't." Shea clutched her chest, feeling her heart hammering against her ribs.

"I said move." Marilyn's patience snapped. She slammed her foot into Shea's side with vicious force.

The kick pushed what little breath she had left from her tortured lungs. White spots danced across her vision as she gasped like a fish out of water.

Lily screamed, the sound echoing off the trees. "She needs help! Please, Marilyn. You've always said you were here to help people find their way."

"Shut up. You chose to deny my help when I offered it." Marilyn pulled plastic zip ties from her pocket and secured the girl to a sturdy oak tree before turning her attention back to Shea. She grabbed the sheriff under the arms and dragged her across the forest floor to drop her next to the creek like a sack of grain.

The cold water lapped at Shea's boots as she lay on the damp tarp. She could hear the stream's cheerful babbling, a sound that should have been peaceful but now seemed like a countdown to her death.

"This will be too easy," Marilyn glared down at her, knife still in hand.

Shea curled in on herself, her hand scrabbling weakly at her jacket. There was supposed to be a spare inhaler in the inner lining—she'd meant to stash one there after her last attack. But her fingers found only fabric and the growing certainty that she was going to die in these woods.

In the distance, she thought she heard someone call her name. Trevor. He was coming.

"You're killing her." Lily sobbed, pulling against the zip ties hard enough to cut into her wrists. "Why? She's done nothing to you. She's trying to help people."

"She ruined my mission." Marilyn pressed her lips together in a thin line. "All those girls I could have saved, all the souls I could have purified. She turned this town against me." She looked down at Shea's struggling form. "I said you can't die yet. I want you to see the end of everything you've tried to protect."

Marilyn reached into her other pocket and pulled out a small, red inhaler. "One of the girls dropped this during her purification. Jennifer, I think. Or maybe it was Sandra—they all fought so hard at first." She tossed it at Shea as if throwing meat to a starving animal. "Remember who is allowing you to breathe."

Shea's fingers closed around the plastic device with desperate gratitude. One puff, then another. The familiar medication began to work its way through her system, slowly convincing her airways to relax. The world stopped spinning quite so violently.

Marilyn pulled out a different knife and sliced through the zip ties binding Lily's wrists. Blood had begun to flow where the plastic had cut into skin. She shoved the girl toward the water's edge.

"Soon, there won't be anyone left to stop me from completing God's work in this town."

~

Trevor watched in horror as Shea stumbled after Marilyn and disappeared into the dense forest. He gripped his weapon so tightly his knuckles went white, every instinct screaming at him to charge after them. But he couldn't rush in blind—that would get them all killed.

He forced himself to think tactically, to push down the panic threatening to overwhelm him. Shea was counting on him to find them, and he wouldn't let her down.

He radioed for Butler to bring Heidi. The dog would be able to track Shea's scent even if Marilyn tried to cover their trail. It was their best hope of finding them before—he refused to complete that thought.

"This is Deputy Bolton requesting immediate assistance. The sheriff has been taken hostage. Bring Heidi to the clearing, now."

"On my way," Butler's voice crackled through the radio. "ETA five minutes."

Five minutes felt like five hours. Trevor paced the edge of the clearing, studying the ground for any sign of which direction they'd gone. Agent Wilson and his partner emerged from their hiding spots, weapons ready.

"We need to move fast," Wilson said. "That woman is completely unhinged."

"Tell me something I don't know." Trevor's voice was tight with worry. He'd never seen Shea have an asthma attack as severe as the one he'd witnessed that morning. If they waited too long, she might not survive even if they rescued her from Marilyn.

It took fifteen agonizing minutes for Heidi to bound into the clearing, Butler close behind. The German Shepherd immediately sensed the urgency, her ears alert and nose already working.

"Find Shea, girl. Hurry." Trevor pointed toward the tree line.

Nose to the ground, the dog darted in the direction Marilyn had taken her captives. Her training kicked in as she followed the scent trail, weaving between trees and underbrush with single-minded determination.

Heidi stopped and sniffed something about a

hundred yards into the trees. Trevor spotted a flash of silver caught on a low branch. He plucked it from the dead pine needles—Shea's badge, deliberately placed where it would catch the light.

Smart girl. Even in the middle of a life-threatening asthma attack, she'd had the presence of mind to leave him a trail to follow.

He tucked the badge into his jacket, jaw clenched with determination, and scanned the woods ahead. He spoke quietly into his radio, knowing the others needed to know the situation.

"This is Deputy Bolton. I've lost visual on the sheriff. She's been taken hostage by Marilyn Townsend. The suspect also has Lily Davidson. I'm following their trail on the old deer path east of Pine Ridge."

A burst of static, then Agent Wilson's voice: "Wait for backup. I repeat, wait for backup. Do not engage alone."

"Shea doesn't have time." Trevor shut off the radio and increased his pace.

He and Heidi moved as fast as they dared through the increasingly difficult terrain, following fleeting clues—scuffs in the dirt, broken branches, a carefully dropped button from Shea's jacket. She was leaving him a trail of breadcrumbs despite her condition.

The path grew narrower and more treacherous as they moved deeper into the forest. Trevor could hear his own heartbeat in his ears, could feel sweat despite the cool morning air. How far ahead were they? How much time did Shea have left?

The dog stopped at the edge of a ridge where the path curved down toward the sound of running water. Over his ragged breathing, Trevor heard it—a woman's voice, then coughing coming from near the creek below.

He put a hand on Heidi's head to keep her from charging ahead. He couldn't afford to give Marilyn any warning that rescue was coming.

"Quiet, girl." Trevor now led the way, staying low and using the trees for cover. Each step had to be deliberate, silent.

Then he saw them.

Shea lay on a tattered tarp next to the water, her face pale and her breathing labored. Marilyn stood over Lily, who was bound to a tree, saying something Trevor couldn't make out from this distance.

Trevor raised his weapon and took aim, then cursed silently as Marilyn crouched down beside Lily. He no longer had a clear shot without risking hitting the girl or Shea.

He closed his eyes and took a deep breath, forcing himself to stay calm. He'd found them, but if he waited too long for the perfect shot, he'd have found them too late.

Time was running out, and Marilyn was getting ready to finish what she'd started.

Chapter Sixteen

Heidi growled low in her throat, the sound vibrated through the forest. Before Trevor could stop her, the dog dashed toward Marilyn with the focused intensity of a predator protecting her pack.

Marilyn dropped the knife with a metallic clatter against the rocks and reached for the gun in her pocket. Too late. Heidi latched onto her arm and gave it a vicious shake, the training Shea had given her taking over completely.

The woman screamed, a sound that echoed off the trees and sent birds scattering from their perches. Her shot went wild, the bullet embedding itself harmlessly in the trunk of an old pine tree.

"Heidi, stop!" Shea pushed to her feet with more strength than she'd felt in the past hour, adrenaline flooding her system as Trevor sprinted past her toward the struggle.

When Marilyn twisted away from the dog and

turned to run, Trevor tackled her to the ground. They went down hard, Marilyn's remaining weapons scattering across the forest floor.

Heidi immediately disengaged and moved to Shea's side, whining softly and looking up at her with concerned dark eyes. The dog's tail wagged uncertainly, as if she wasn't sure whether she'd done the right thing.

"I'm okay, girl." Shea ran her hand through the dog's thick fur, feeling the tremor in her own fingers as the crisis passed. And she was okay, but she had come very close to dying that day. Too close.

"Get off me!" Marilyn struggled under Trevor's weight, her face pressed into the damp earth and leaves. "You may have stopped me, but someone will take my place. You watch and see. There are others who understand what needs to be done in this godforsaken town."

"Then we'll take them down, too." Trevor hauled her to her feet with more force than strictly necessary. "One at a time if we have to."

Deputy Butler and the two FBI agents burst into the clearing, weapons drawn and breathing hard from their sprint through the woods. Agent Snowe immediately moved to secure the scene while Larson approached with handcuffs.

Trevor glared their way. "Thanks for the backup, but I've got this. No help to you."

"We told you to wait for support," Agent Larson said, his voice carrying the authority of federal jurisdiction and wounded pride.

"Lily would be dead if he'd waited." Shea's chest still ached from the recent asthma attack, each breath a conscious effort, but she'd live. More importantly, so would Lily Davidson. "Me, too, most likely."

Agent Larson stepped forward to take custody of Marilyn, who continued to mutter under her breath about divine missions and corrupted souls. "We'll need full statements from both of you."

"Later," Trevor said firmly. "Shea needs to get to the clinic and have her breathing regulated." He handed Marilyn over to the agents with obvious reluctance. "We'll meet you at the station afterward to fill out the reports."

He took Shea's hand, his fingers warm and steady against her still-trembling ones, and led her away from the others. Behind them, Agent Larson read Marilyn her rights while she continued to rant about purification and salvation.

"I really don't need to go to the clinic now," Shea protested, though her voice still carried the raspy quality that said otherwise. "I can breathe fine."

"Well, I need you to go." He stopped walking and faced her, his expression more serious than she'd ever seen it. "You've put me in some scary situations before, Shea, but today... I thought I was going to find you dead."

She started to protest, but he continued before she could speak.

"When I was tracking you through these woods, listening to Heidi whine because she'd lost your scent at the creek, I kept thinking about what I'd do if I was too late." He cupped her face in his hands, his thumbs brushing across her cheekbones. "I couldn't have survived that."

Her gaze searched his face, seeing vulnerability she'd never noticed before. "Trevor..."

"When I thought today might be the end for you, I realized something important. Something I should have said a long time ago."

"What?" Her breath caught, and for once it had nothing to do with her medical condition.

"Whether you feel the same or not, I have to say this because I might not get another chance." His voice was steady despite the emotion behind it. "I love you, Shea. I love you because you're strong and fearless, because you're brave even when the odds are stacked against you. But most of all, no matter the circumstances, you always do the right thing for the people of this town. For me."

Tears stung her eyes, blurring her vision. The words she'd been afraid to hear, afraid to hope for, hung in the air between them like a bridge she was terrified to cross.

"I can't, Trevor." The words came out broken, barely a whisper. "Everyone I care about dies. Everyone I let get close gets hurt."

"Not everyone." He stepped back but didn't release

her hands. "I know you lost someone up on that mountain, but you've saved all the others since then. You've saved me, more times than you know."

She wanted to tell him she felt the same, that she'd been fighting her feelings for him for months. But voicing the words felt like putting a target on his back. Someone out there with a vengeance against her would eventually go after him, just like they always went after the people she cared about.

"I'm not asking for promises, Shea," he said softly, as if reading her thoughts. "I just want you to know that I'm here for as long as it takes. For whatever you need."

Instead of the words that wanted to pour out of her heart, she simply nodded and followed him down the deer trail out of the woods.

By noon, word had spread through Misty Hollow about the arrest of Marilyn and Mark Townsend like wildfire through dry grass. Some mourned who they thought the couple had been—pillars of the community, servants of God. Others were outraged that such evil had hidden behind religious authority for so long.

Shea succumbed to Trevor's insistence and paid a visit to the clinic, where a doctor administered a steroid shot and prescribed medication to help return her breathing to normal. It warmed her heart and frightened her in equal measure that Trevor cared so much, that he wanted to take care of her.

She'd worked hard her entire adult life to not have to depend on anyone. Independence had been her armor against loss and disappointment. But if she was being honest with herself, she did depend on Trevor—to always be there for her, to always have her back, to understand the weight she carried as sheriff of this complicated town.

Now, as the sun set over Misty Lake in brilliant shades of orange and pink, and Heidi sniffed contentedly at the bushes along the shore, Shea stared out over the water. It was a beautiful place, this lake that had been home to so much death and sorrow.

She lowered herself to a large boulder near where Abby Pearson's body had been found just days ago. The world around her started to settle into evening quiet. Birds hushed their day songs, the water lapped gently at the shore as a cool breeze stirred the surface. From somewhere in the distance, the low hum of a boat engine cut off, leaving only the natural sounds of the wilderness.

Shea breathed in deep and steady, grateful for lungs that worked properly again. Heidi wandered over and sat next to her, nudging her hand with a wet nose as if to say everything would be okay now.

With a sigh that carried the weight of the past few weeks, she stood and turned toward the parking lot. Toward home. Toward whatever came next with Trevor, if she could find the courage to accept what he was offering.

When she reached her truck, she cast one more look at the lake, its surface now reflecting the first stars of evening.

It didn't speak, but she knew it would remember everything—the victims, the killer. No, the lake wouldn't forget and neither would Shea.

The End

Dear Reader,

If you enjoyed *Drowned in Silence*, please visit Amazon and leave a review. Reviews are a writer's lifeline. Thank you.

Cynthia

www.cynthiahickey.com

Cynthia Hickey is a multi-published and best-selling author of cozy mysteries and romantic suspense/thrillers. She has taught writing at many conferences and small writing retreats. She and her husband run the publishing press, Winged Publications. They live in Arizona and Arkansas, becoming snowbirds with three dogs. They have ten grandchildren who keep them busy and tell everyone they know that "Nana is a writer."

Connect with me on <u>FaceBook</u>
<u>Twitter</u>
Sign up for my <u>newsletter and receive a free short story</u>

<u>www.cynthiahickey.com</u>

Follow me on <u>Amazon</u>
And <u>Bookbub</u>
Shop my bookstore <u>on shopify</u>. For better price and autographed books.

Enjoy other books by Cynthia Hickey

The Sheriff of Misty Hollow
<u>Girls' Weekend Survival</u>
<u>The Threat</u>
<u>Evil Returns</u>

Cowboys of Misty Hollow
<u>Cowboy Jeopardy</u>
<u>Cowboy Peril</u>
<u>Cowboy Hazard</u>
<u>Cowgirl Blaze</u>
<u>Cowboy Uncertainty</u>
<u>Cowboy Christmas Crisis</u>
<u>Cowboy Pitfall</u>

Misty Hollow
Secrets of Misty Hollow
Deceptive Peace
Calm Surface
Lightning Never Strikes Twice
Lethal Inheritance
Bitter Isolation
Say I Don't
Christmas Stalker
Bridge to Safety
When Night Falls
A Place to Hide
Mountain Refuge

Stay in Misty Hollow for a while. Get the entire series here!

The Seven Deadly Sins series
Deadly Pride
Deadly Covet
Deadly Lust
Deadly Glutton
Deadly Envy
Deadly Sloth
Deadly Anger

The Tail Waggin' Mysteries
Cat-Eyed Witness
The Dog Who Found a Body

A Strange Game for Caper
Caper Steals Christmas
Caper Finds a Treasure
Tiny House Mysteries boxed set

Wife for Hire – Private Investigators
Saving Sarah
Lesson for Lacey
Mission for Meghan
Long Way for Lainie
Aimed at Amy
Wife for Hire (all five in one)

A Hollywood Murder
Killer Pose, book 1
Killer Snapshot, book 2
Shoot to Kill, book 3
Kodak Kill Shot, book 4
To Snap a Killer
Hollywood Murder Mysteries

Shady Acres Mysteries
Beware the Orchids, book 1
Path to Nowhere
Poison Foliage
Poinsettia Madness
Deadly Greenhouse Gases
Vine Entrapment
Shady Acres Boxed Set

CLEAN BUT GRITTY Romantic Suspense

Highland Springs

Murder Live
Say Bye to Mommy
To Breathe Again
Highland Springs Murders (all 3 in one)

Colors of Evil Series

Shades of Crimson
Coral Shadows

The Pretty Must Die Series

Ripped in Red, book 1
Pierced in Pink, book 2
Wounded in White, book 3
Worthy, The Complete Story

Lisa Paxton Mystery Series

Eenie Meenie Miny Mo
Jack Be Nimble
Hickory Dickory Dock
Boxed Set

Hearts of Courage
A Heart of Valor

The Game
Suspicious Minds
After the Storm
Local Betrayal
Hearts of Courage Boxed Set

Overcoming Evil series
Mistaken Assassin
Captured Innocence
Mountain of Fear
Exposure at Sea
A Secret to Die for
Collision Course
Romantic Suspense of 5 books in 1

* 9 7 8 1 9 6 5 3 5 2 9 8 4 *